MY WOUNDED
BILLIONAIRE

by

SERENITY WOODS

DEDICATION

To Tony & Chris, my Kiwi boys.

CONTENTS

Prologue

Saturday, 8 June

The night of the cyclone

Fitz

I leave the sanctuary of the Ark and head out into the wildness of the winter night.

Man, it's crazy out here. The wind is blowing so hard, it's impossible to stand upright. I double over, clutching my jacket around me, and stagger toward the petting farm across the field from the main block. I should have had my hair cut; it's getting long, curling like a bastard, and the wind whips it around my face and makes it sting.

I hope Poppy doesn't mind me joining her at the petting farm. I don't like the idea of her staying there alone during the storm. She'll be trying to keep all the animals calm, and it's scary enough with every plank of wood and loose tile flapping and banging about, without having to worry about the goats and rabbits getting twitchy.

My decision to head over there has nothing to do with the fact that I find her attractive. That I take any opportunity I can get to spend time around her, so I can listen to her soft, slightly husky voice when she talks, and study her slender figure when she's not looking.

I've been building up to asking her out for a while. She hasn't been at the Ark that long—only three or four months. She was a primary school teacher, but her brother, Albie, told me that she had a relationship with one of the deputy principals, and it ended badly.

SERENITY WOODS

Because of this, I've given her a little space, but I don't want to leave it too long and see her snapped up by someone else.

I reach the enclosure, which is empty, all the animals obviously inside the barn. Poppy appears to have chained the gate with a padlock to ensure it doesn't come loose, so I attempt to vault over the fence, catch my foot on one of the planks, and end up on my backside on the ground.

Swearing under my breath, I get up and dust myself down, stumble across to the barn, push the door hard, and pitch headfirst into the barn onto the floor again.

"Hello, Mr. Elegant." Poppy closes the door behind me, puts a bar across it, and offers me a hand. "Are you auditioning for *Dancing with the Stars?*"

I scowl, take her hand, and let her pull me to my feet. She's surprisingly strong considering she's six inches shorter than me and about thirty pounds lighter.

"My back doesn't bend the way it used to," I tell her. "I forget sometimes." An accident injured my spine when I was in the Army. I've had surgery, but the injury has never healed completely—a constant reminder that I'm thirty-two now and only half the man I used to be.

"What are you doing over here?" She tucks a strand of her long curly hair behind her ear. It's a beautiful auburn color, like trees in autumn, their leaves about to fall. "You took your life in your hands venturing out into this weather."

"I wanted to check you were all right," I tell her. "I didn't like the idea of you being alone."

She gives me a wry look. "I'm not a maiden in distress. I don't need saving."

"I know."

She meets my gaze for a moment. Then she drops hers and goes to lean on the wall that surrounds the animals. I join her, our arms a few inches apart. The animals are quiet at the moment, and don't seem too worried about the rattling of the rafters.

"Where's Jack?" she asks, referring to the Jack Russell who's usually by my side.

"Back at the Ark. I didn't want to bring him out in this weather."

"Any news on the cyclone?"

"We're in the middle of it now. I think we can expect another couple of hours of this."

She nods. "I brought a sleeping bag. I thought I might stay the night, just in case the animals are frightened."

"I'll stay with you, if you like."

Her green-eyed gaze comes back to me again. "You don't need to do that."

"I know." I take a deep breath. Time to show my hand. "I want to spend some time with you. Is that so surprising to you?"

Her eyes widen. Albie told me she doesn't get subtlety, and that she won't believe I'm interested unless I say it straight up—that she would think I'm just being polite when I try to talk to her, and I realize he was right.

She swallows, then looks away and clears her throat. "Want a drink?" she asks eventually. "I've got some whisky in the office."

"Sure," I say, relieved she hasn't thrown me out.

She heads over to the offices next to the barn, and I follow her. She's just rummaging in one of the drawers when all the lights go out.

"Shit!" She jumps.

"Christ. Hold on." I pull out my phone and switch on the built-in flashlight. "I should have brought a torch with me—that was always going to happen."

"I think I've got one in the cupboard by the sink." With me shining the light on the drawers, she retrieves the whisky bottle, then brings it over to the small kitchen. She finds the flashlight in the cupboard and hands it to me, then retrieves two glasses and pours a small measure of whisky into them.

She hands one to me. I hold it up. "To world peace."

Her lips curve up and she gives a husky chuckle. Wow, that sent a shiver all the way down my spine. "To world peace," she repeats, tapping her glass to mine.

We take a sip, and then, carrying the whisky bottle, she leads the way back into the barn. At one end, she's spread out a blanket and her sleeping bag, and we go there and slide down the wall onto the blanket.

"Whisky's pretty good," I say. "Canadian?"

"Yes. How did you know?"

"I could tell from the notes of treacle and burnt ash."

"Really?"

"No, I read the label." I gesture to where it's sitting in the straw to one side, and she laughs.

"Yeah," she says, "that's a bit of a giveaway. So you're not a whisky connoisseur then?"

"When the budget allows." I bite my tongue. Poppy's a member of the wealthy King family, and I don't want to draw attention to the fact that she has money and I don't. "I like the Islay malts," I tell her, hoping to distract her. "Ardbeg, Lagavulin, and Laphroaig, especially."

"And if you don't drink it all, you can always use it to wash any wounds," she says.

I grin. "It does have a strong, medicinal smell."

"It's definitely an acquired taste."

We sit in the quiet for a while, listening to the wind howling around us. Occasionally boards rattle, but I did a check around the farm this morning, nailing down anything loose, and so far it seems to be holding.

I look across at her. She's studying a piece of straw, twirling it in her fingers. I think she's doing it so she doesn't have to look at me. I know she's thirty, and I'm two years older, but it feels as if we're a couple of teenagers.

"I should have brought a book over," I say. "I could have read to you."

"What are you reading at the moment?"

I name the series of thrillers I've recently got into. She's also read the first two, so we spend a pleasant few minutes talking about the plots and characters, and then we discuss the movie version.

It's the first time we've spoken like this, on our own, without anyone else listening in. Previously we've always been in a group, or chatting in the square, with people walking past. She's softly spoken, and up close like this I can see how she considers each question thoughtfully.

I want to get to know her better, to spend more time with her like this. To find out her likes and dislikes, her hopes and dreams. I want to make her laugh again, to have her nudge me the way she just did, to have her tease me, her eyes look up into mine with admiration and longing. I want to kiss her. I've wanted to kiss her for a long time.

"So," I say, aware I have to broach the subject eventually. "Maybe tomorrow, when the storm is over. How do you fancy coming to dinner with me?"

She lifts her gaze to mine. Her eyes glitter in the beam from the flashlight.

"Marc…" she whispers.

"I like you," I tell her. "I have since the first moment I laid eyes on you. But Albie said you'd had a bad breakup, so I waited for a bit. I didn't want to push you. But it's been a few months now, and… well… I didn't want to wait any longer."

She scratches at a mark on her jeans. "I'm very flattered."

Jesus. She's going to say no.

"But I'm not interested," she finishes, confirming my fears.

"May I ask why?"

"I'm not interested in having another relationship."

My eyebrows rise. "Never?"

"No. It's too hard." Her brow furrows. "I'm not made to be with someone else."

Now my frown matches hers. "That's bullshit. Of course you are."

"No, I'm not. My brain doesn't work the same way as everyone else's. People communicate in a different way than me, and I don't understand them." Her tone is sharp, her voice harsh. "And I'm done with being criticized for it. I don't want the hassle. I don't need a man. I like you, Marc, and I'm so touched that you're interested in me, but you don't know the real me."

"I'd like to."

"Thank you, but the answer's no. I'm done with dating."

And that's that. She's turned me down. I can't force her to go out with me. I can't make her understand that she deserves happiness, and if she were to be my girl, I'd make sure to wipe all thoughts of her ex from her mind.

She rubs her nose. "You should go," she says. Her voice is little more than a squeak. "Before the weather gets any worse." She thinks that now she's turned me down, I'm not going to want to stay with her.

I gesture toward the bottle of whisky resting in the straw. "When there's whisky on offer? I don't think so. You're stuck with me tonight."

She lifts her gaze to mine, confused, a little tearful. "You heard what I said?" she confirms. "I don't want to date."

"I heard you. Doesn't mean we can't be friends. And I'm not leaving you alone tonight."

She looks away. Her bottom lip trembles briefly. I wish I could pull her into my arms and hug her, make her feel better, but I can't. All I can do is sit here and talk. And wait. Who knows, maybe one day she'll finally be over her ex, and when she is, I'll be ready.

"Pass the bottle," I say. "Let's get drunk."

She looks back at me and swallows hard. "You can stay if you like," she says. "But you're not sharing my sleeping bag."

"Spoilsport." I take the bottle from her and pour us both another shot. "To friendship."

"To friendship," she whispers, and we both have a mouthful of the whisky.

Chapter One

Four months later

Poppy

The little girl at the back of the group of pre-school children stays behind as the rest of them leave the rabbits and head outside. She gives me a hesitant smile.

"Hello." I drop to my haunches and smile back. She's holding a toy bunny under her arm, well-loved, its white fur now a dull gray, its left ear frayed where she obviously chews it. I gesture at it. "What a gorgeous bunny. Are rabbits your favorite animals?"

She nods and glances past me at the pen where six rabbits are chewing contentedly at their pellets—two English angoras, three New Zealand whites, and a beautiful French Lop.

"Would you like to hold one?" I ask her. While the rest of the class had passed the rabbits around, she'd sat at the back, too shy to come forward, but now she nods, her beautiful blue eyes lighting up. "Come and sit down," I say, and then I pass her one of the whites, which sits in her arms quite happily as she strokes its back, her eyes sparkling.

I watch her, smiling, thinking how beautiful she is. She must be about four years old. She has the most gorgeous blonde hair that hangs like a shining curtain. I'd kill for hair like that. My auburn curly hair always looks as if I've stuck my fingers in an electric plug, and when it gets humid in summer it doubles in volume.

If I had a little girl, would she look like this? Or would she inherit my mad hair?

"Aimee," the teacher calls out. "Come on, it's time to go."

Aimee gives me the rabbit back reluctantly and slips her hand into mine as I lead her out of the shed toward the bus parked in front of the petting farm. Oh, she's so sweet. Her mother must be so thrilled to have such a beautiful daughter.

There's a man over by the fence, in the process of nailing one of the planks back in place where it had slipped. He looks up as we pass. It's Marc Fitzgerald—the Ark's estate manager. I glance at him, and my gaze snags as if caught on a nail as I see what he's wearing. Normally, he dons a suit for work, as he often has meetings with the architects or the building contractors. Today, though, as he's doing some maintenance, he's changed into a pair of coveralls. It's the first of October, so technically not close to summer yet, but up here in the sub-tropical Northland it's always hot by lunchtime, and he's peeled off the top part of the coveralls, tying the arms around his waist. He's bare-chested, and a little sweaty. His skin is gleaming in the sunshine like honed and varnished wood. He has curly hair, like me, but his is dark and normally skims his collar, and he hasn't shaved in a while. He's *scruffy as*. But it doesn't hide the fact that he's in fine shape, a perfect specimen of manliness.

I'm pretty sure he's taken his top off for my benefit. It wouldn't surprise me if he sprayed himself with water to enhance his shiny muscles. The man is relentless.

Four months ago, during the cyclone that destroyed part of the Ark, he spent the evening with me at the petting farm, looking after the animals. In the midst of the power outage, when the lights went out and we were sitting in the dark in the straw, he asked me out. I said no thank you, I wasn't interested in a relationship, and assumed that would be the end of it—he'd keep to his side of the Ark, and I'd keep to mine, and never the twain shall meet. I thought that days later I'd see him dating another girl. But he hasn't. He comes over all the time, and actually we've kinda become good friends. Which is why I'm approaching him today with a specific request in mind.

He bends over to pick up a piece of wood, the coveralls clinging to his neat butt. I tear my gaze away before I walk into something, and return Aimee to her teacher.

"Thank you for an amazing afternoon," the teacher says as Aimee boards the bus. "This is such a cool idea. The talk you gave them about caring for animals was really well done."

"Thank you," I reply, taken aback by her praise. "I appreciate you saying that."

One of the purposes of the petting farm is to teach children of all ages to respect animals. Children are rarely cruel by nature; if they do hurt an animal, it's usually because they've seen someone in their family be violent toward another person or animal. If I can help even one child turn away from that behavioral programming, I'll consider it a job well done.

I wave goodbye as the bus pulls away, feeling an inner glow. Phew, it's warm. I have an hour now before there's another class visit, so it's time for a cool drink and some lunch.

Turning, I glance over at Marc. His Jack Russell, called—rather unimaginatively—Jack, and who's almost always by his side, sniffs around in the grass. Marc's collecting up his tools, but I have a feeling he was watching me. Today, though, I don't mind, as I wanted to talk to him.

"Warm afternoon, isn't it?" I say as I walk up to the fence. I poke my fingers through for Jack to lick.

Marc straightens and nods. The hollow at the base of his throat gleams with moisture. "Summer's on its way."

I try not to stare at the stubble on his jaw. "I can't wait. Noah said he's having a pool put in, did he tell you? We'll be able to use it during our lunch hour." I bet Marc looks good in swim shorts.

"Yeah, that'll be brilliant," he says. "Swimming is good exercise; it takes your weight off your joints."

"Your back bothering you?" I know he was wounded when he was in the Army—he served for a while at Scott Base in Antarctica, and he injured his spine when a plane crash-landed. He still walks stiffly, and sometimes I see him arching his back where it's obviously paining him.

He bends and zips up his tool bag. "Sometimes." He straightens, the bag in his hands. "Well, I suppose I'd better get back to work."

I take a deep breath. Am I really going to do this? I've been thinking about it for weeks—months, actually, ever since he asked me out. I have no idea what he's going to say. He might laugh and go back to the Ark and tell everyone, or get angry and ask me what the hell I'm thinking. Neither would surprise me.

Still, nothing ventured...

"I was just going to have some lunch and a cold drink," I tell him. "Would you like to join me?"

He stares at me, obviously taken aback. I wait, expecting a rejection. But he just says, "Okay," walks over and places his tool bag by his Ford

Ranger Raptor—what Kiwis call a 'ute' or utility vehicle and Americans call a truck—clicks his fingers at Jack to follow him, then crosses the yard and follows me inside.

I'm lucky enough to work in a beautiful office. Usually, I share it with Sandra or Rachel, the two women who work shifts, helping me out with the animals, but today I'm on my own, and the office is empty. Its front windows look out over the fields and the valley beyond, and it's filled with sunshine. The back windows face the Ark. As I glance out, I can see Leon and Nix walking across the square, heading for the office block. A woman has arrived with a scruffy terrier, ready to have it washed and trimmed in the brand-new grooming rooms. In the distance, I can see Noah, walking with his girlfriend, his two German Shepherds bouncing around the stroller he's pushing that contains his new baby boy.

I turn away and walk over to the small kitchen in the corner, and take out a couple of cans of Sprite Zero from the fridge. I show them to Marc, who nods, and then add some ice to two tall glasses and pour the Sprite over them. He comes and collects them as I put a bowl of water down for Jack, along with a dog biscuit. Then I take out the box of bread rolls from the fridge and bring them over to the small table by the window.

"Do you mind if I leave this off?" Marc gestures to the top of his coveralls. "I'm a bit hot after working on the fence."

"Not at all." I glance up and meet his eyes briefly. I can smell his warmed body spray from here. It makes my mouth water. I drop my gaze to the box and remove the lid. "Chicken salad or ham and mayonnaise?"

"Ham, please."

I take one out and pass it to him, and I choose a chicken one. We both take a bite and munch away.

"So..." He has a swig from the glass of Sprite, then wipes his mouth on the back of his hand. "To what do I owe this honor?" His eyes gleam with amusement as he has another bite of his roll.

I shrug. "You were working hard, and I thought you were probably hungry."

"I'm always hungry. But that doesn't explain why you made extra rolls for lunch today."

He's got me there. I'd done so in the hope that I'd spot him around the grounds. "All right," I scold him. "Enough with the third degree. Yes, I planned this."

His lips curve up. "Okay." He sits back in his chair and studies me, eating his roll in another two bites. He has the perfect amount of chest hair—not too much so he's like a gorilla, but enough to illustrate his masculinity. He works outside a lot, so his skin is very brown all over. Well, almost all over. I wouldn't imagine he's tanned down there...

I lift my gaze to his. There's laughter in his eyes, as if he's able to read my mind.

"You look lovely today, by the way," he says softly.

I blink a few times, taken aback by a second compliment in almost as many minutes. "Oh. Thank you."

"That color suits you." He gestures at my orange T-shirt. "It goes with your hair." His gaze caresses it. And then, I realize what he's thinking, what he's concluded from my asking him here for lunch. Shit.

"I haven't changed my mind," I tell him, as gently as I can. "About going out with you."

His smile fades, to be replaced with a frown. He turns the glass around in his fingers before returning his gaze to me.

"Why?" he asks.

That stumps me.

"I told you last time, I don't want a relationship," I remind him.

"You don't want a relationship with me? Or with anyone?"

I take a piece of lettuce out of the roll. It's soggy, and I don't like soggy lettuce. "With anyone."

"Is this to do with Daniel?"

I give him a sharp look. How much does he know about my ex? I broke up with Daniel last Christmas. The only person I told what happened was my brother, Albie...

I sigh. Albie can't keep a secret to save his life. No doubt he's told the whole of the Ark by now.

"That's irrelevant," I tell Marc, lifting my chin.

"It's not," he states. "You've been hurt badly, I can see that. And I understand why it's making you feel that you don't want to get involved with anyone again. But you can't let a fucking idiot like that ruin the rest of your life."

His description of Daniel brings a small smile to my face. "I appreciate your concern," I tell him. "But as I said, that's irrelevant. That's not why I asked you in today."

He doesn't like the answer. He narrows his eyes and glares at me. But he doesn't push the matter. "All right," he says. "So why did you ask me in?"

I lean forward on the table and examine my hands for a moment. "I'm wondering if you can help me out."

"Of course," he says. "Anything."

I give him a wry look. "I think you'd better wait and see what I want first."

"Okay…"

I take a deep breath and finally reveal the dream that's been on my mind, and in my heart, for a long, long time. "I want a baby."

Chapter Two

Fitz

I stare at Poppy. "What?"

"I want a baby," she repeats, finally meeting my eyes. There's a look of steely determination in them. She's not joking. She means it.

"I'm confused," I tell her. "You want me to kidnap you one or something?"

"No, Marc," she says, slightly exasperated. Even though everyone else at the Ark calls me Fitz, she's always called me Marc. "I'm asking you whether you would agree to being a sperm donor."

I'm so taken aback I can't think what to say. If you'd asked me to guess what she was going to come out with, this would have been at the very bottom of the list. Probably not on the list at all, in fact.

The beautiful woman sitting before me chews her bottom lip. For the first time, she looks unsure, maybe even wary. She's worried about how I'm going to react. I'm not surprised. I'm not sure how I'm going to react.

Because I'm not sure what to say, I don't say anything. Instead, I sit and study her for a while. My God, she's beautiful. I know she turned thirty back in March, but she has flawless skin and a slim figure, and she looks five years younger. I wish she'd said yes to a date, but I know her ex killed her confidence. Albie admitted Daniel said some incredibly cruel things to her.

Like Albie, and their father, Charlie, Poppy's on the spectrum, and obviously struggles with communication and social issues. Because of this, she's extremely quiet, and possibly the most private person I've ever met. Although she's happy to chat to me, she rarely shares details of herself, and even though I've known her for a while now, most of the information I've gleaned about her has come from the other members of her family.

SERENITY WOODS

Albie told me that Daniel accused her of being a frigid ice queen who shouldn't be allowed out into society. I don't know what prompted him to say that; I suspect he didn't understand that although she might not always show emotion, she does feel it. And that if her feelings are hurt, she undoubtedly withdraws. Frigid implies something went wrong in bed, too, but I sincerely doubt she was passionless. Nobody with eyes as expressive as hers has a lack of passion in her soul.

I'd really hoped that as time went by, she might come around to the idea of dating me. But instead, she's come out with this. She wants me to father her child.

I'm a confusing mixture of flattered and puzzled. Part of me understands why she's made this decision. She's been hurt, and she doesn't want to enter into another relationship, but she obviously wants children, so she's decided that being inseminated by a sperm donor is the best method.

But she's chosen me. Out of all the guys she knows.

"Why?" I ask, baffled.

"Why do I want a baby?" she clarifies.

"No. I mean, Christ, why on earth do you want me? I can't imagine any woman choosing me to be the father of their baby. Why not just go to a sperm bank?"

She shrugs. "I looked into it, and it's definitely an option. But I'd feel more comfortable if the father was someone I knew." Her gaze slips down me, making me tingle as if she's using the tips of her fingers. "I like you. You're an excellent physical specimen. You're tall and good looking. You're strong and you seem healthy. You're intelligent, kind, honest, and loyal. Those are the kinds of traits I'd be happy to reproduce in my children."

I'm close to blushing. No woman has ever said anything remotely like that to me before.

Equally, I'm so disappointed I feel an ache deep inside. "Honey," I tell her, "I'm incredibly flattered, unless you've already debated everyone else and I'm the last on the list."

"You're not," she says. "You've always been at the top."

I give a short laugh and look out of the window. She actually has a good sense of humor, but sometimes she misses sarcasm and irony, and she says exactly what's on her mind. "It must be a very short list."

"Not at all. Why don't you think you'd be an attractive proposition?"

I don't know how to answer that. I look back at her. "Well…" I say carefully, "as I said, I'm very flattered, but it seems such a waste. You should be dating, whether it's me or someone else. You never know, it might work out, and then the whole baby thing might happen of its own accord."

But she shakes her head, determined. "No. I'm not made to be in a relationship."

"Aw, Poppy…"

She holds up a hand. "It's just the way it is. I don't understand men, and I'm terrible at being a partner. And I'm not going through it again. I'm done. But I do want children."

"How many are we having?"

She glares at me. "Are you making fun of me?"

"Not at all."

"Well, we could start with one and see how it goes."

"Right." I stretch out my legs, fold my hands, and tip my head to one side as I study her. "So how would this work, then?"

"You want me to explain artificial insemination?"

"No. I'd like some more details on how I would be involved."

"You don't need to be involved at all. Other than… you know… the obvious."

"What if I want to be?"

She hesitates. "Well… um…" She frowns. "I'd assumed you wouldn't be interested. I thought you'd be relieved not to be involved. In my experience, the last thing men are interested in is commitment."

She's talking about Daniel again. He wouldn't commit to her. Maybe she mentioned wanting children and he said no. Anger flares inside me. "So what do I get out of it?" I ask her. I'm being sarcastic, but she doesn't pick up on it.

"I'd pay you," she says. "A thousand dollars for each… donation."

"Jesus." She thinks I'd take money from her for jerking off into a cup. She thinks she has to pay me to get me to help her.

My frustration flows over. Before I say something I'll regret, I stand up. "I'm sorry, I've got things to do."

"But—"

I walk out before she can finish, snapping at Jack to follow me, go over to the car, plonk Jack on the passenger seat, throw the tool bag in the back, and drive away.

I'm so angry, I want to hit something. I'm tempted to drive into Paihia to the local primary school, find Daniel Magget—or the Maggot, as I call him—and beat the living shit out of him. Fucking bastard. I bang the steering wheel. He's spoiled her, corrupted the soul I know gleams like gold beneath her current layer of hurt and pain.

I drive into the Ark's car park, get out, and stride across with Jack at my heels to the office block.

"Hey." Albie lifts a hand in greeting as I pass, but I ignore him and walk through to my office. I slam the door, making the whole building rattle. Jack goes under the table and lies with his snout on his paws.

"Stupid fucking idiot," I mumble, unzipping the bottom half of my coveralls and stepping out of them. I pull on my suit pants, take out a can of deodorant from my desk, and spray under my arms before I pull on my shirt.

I turn as there's a knock at the door, and Albie sticks his head around. "You okay?" he asks. "You looked… upset." Jack goes over to him as if to say *Albie, Fitz is in one of his moods again!*

I put my hands on my hips and glower at him. "I've just been talking to Poppy."

He comes in and slides his hands into his pockets. "Yeah, she can be frustrating."

"I'm not frustrated with her. I'm angry with Daniel-fucking-Maggot-head."

His lips curve up. "Ah."

I turn and throw my coveralls into the corner of the room. "I want to strangle him."

"You'll have to get in line, I'm afraid. Dad and I are in front."

It must have been bad if both Albie and Charlie King are feeling physical toward him. "He hurt her," I whisper. "Badly."

"I know."

"She won't go out with me because of him."

Albie sighs and studies his feet. "I'm sorry."

"I don't know how to persuade her that I'm not like him."

"You'll just have to give her time," he says softly.

I blow out a long breath. "And I'd be happy to do that, except she's just asked me…"

His eyebrows rise. "What?"

I look out of the window. I shouldn't betray her confidence. But I honestly have nobody else to talk to about it. And if anyone has an idea of how to navigate the minefield that is Poppy's mind, it's her brother.

I look back at him. "She's just asked me whether I would be a sperm donor for a baby."

Albie stares at me. "What?"

"I know."

"Jesus."

"Yeah." I run a hand through my hair.

"Was she serious?"

"Oh yes. And the thing I'm worried about most is that if I say no, she's going to go ahead and do it anyway. Go to a sperm bank or something."

I'd half expected Albie to laugh, but he sits on the edge of the desk, looking pained. "She wants kids," he says.

"Looks that way."

"It's because she turned thirty."

"I'm guessing. And what happened with Daniel has convinced her she's not going to have a successful relationship, so she's got to do it this way."

He studies me. "What did you say?"

"I walked out. I was frustrated and I didn't want to say something I regretted." I sigh. It was rude of me, and she deserves better. It must have taken her a lot of courage to ask me. "I'll go back in a while and apologize."

"Are you going to agree?"

I frown. "I don't know. It's a bit odd, fathering a child I'd then have no connection with. I don't think she'd want me to be around for it. And she obviously doesn't need child support." As a King, Poppy is already very rich. "But if she's serious…" I'm puzzled. I can't work out my feelings on this. I feel flattered and resentful and angry and oddly hopeful, all rolled into one. "She offered to pay me," I say, and roll my eyes.

Albie shrugs. "You'd get paid if you donated to a sperm bank."

I stare at him. "Are you saying you agree with it?"

"I'm saying she wants a child, and you're her friend, and ultimately it's not a huge task for you to do something that will make her incredibly happy. I'm sure she didn't mean to offend you by offering money. She probably thought it would make it feel more like a transaction, and that you'd be pleased."

I hadn't considered that. Maybe she'd be horrified to think she'd offended me. I tuck my shirt in my trousers, mumbling under my breath.

"You really like her, don't you?" Albie says.

I scratch my cheek, my nails rasping on bristle. I need a shave. "I wish I could convince her to go out with me and do this the normal way."

"If you can't," Albie says, getting up as his mobile rings, "you might just have to be inventive." He winks at me, gives Jack a final pat, and walks out as he answers his phone.

I sit, put my feet up on the table, and lean back in my chair. Poppy has another couple of classes visiting now, so there's no point me going over there for a while. It'll give me time to think about it, at least.

What on earth am I going to say to her?

My instinct is to say no. But I'm ashamed to admit I am tempted, and the reason is actually nothing to do with Poppy. The reason is that I need the money, and Poppy is offering to pay me for a service that, as Albie said, isn't a huge task for me. It would make her happy. So why am I balking?

I suppose it's the weird notion of fathering a child in secret. I presume she wouldn't want to tell either the child or everyone else here who the father was. I shouldn't have told Albie. I'll have to have a word with him to keep his mouth shut.

If I say no, she may well go ahead via a sperm bank if she's desperate for a child, and it appears she is to even be considering the option.

I don't want her to get pregnant by another man.

The realization is somewhat startling. I'd rather make her happy by helping her to get pregnant than let her go through it all alone, using some stranger's sperm.

Wow. What a bizarre eureka moment. I never thought when I woke up this morning that I'd be thinking about fathering a child.

The thought fills me with a strange warmth. Before my father died, my childhood was run-of-the-mill, neither good nor bad, although that all changed after Dad died when I was fifteen. Mom's alcoholism and unhappiness meant my late teens were difficult, and I was glad to get away. The Army provided the security and stability I'd missed, until it was ripped away from me by the accident. My relationships have all ended somewhat disastrously, especially the last one. Sometimes, I've thought it's unlikely I'll ever settle down and have a family. So the thought of getting Poppy pregnant is strangely appealing.

The thing is, I don't just want to father her children. I want to do more than physically inseminate her. I want the whole kit and caboodle. I want her.

I stare off across the fields. *You might have to be inventive…*

What if there was a way to help her out, *and* get what I want? She likes me. She must do. Her compliments proved that. And anyway, she wouldn't ask a man she has no feelings for to father her child, surely.

You're an excellent physical specimen. You're tall and good looking. You're strong and you seem healthy. You're intelligent, kind, honest, and loyal.

I doodle on a notepad. I've spent most of this year chasing her, trying to get her to go out with me. What the hell. Do I really have to think this hard about it?

As a plan begins to formulate in my mind, I pull up a browser on my computer, and start doing some research.

Chapter Three

Poppy

It's a long afternoon with two difficult classes of children who are poorly controlled by their young teachers, and who, as a consequence, run amok amongst the animals. I don't like to take over from the teachers, even if I think I could do better, because I know teaching is a really hard job, and undermining someone else is the worst thing you can do for their self-respect. But when the noise level frightens a couple of the new puppies, I end up losing my temper and taking half a dozen of the badly behaved kids out of the farm and into the office, where I give them a solid talking to about respect. I make two of them cry, and feel a swathe of guilt, until their teacher comes up afterward and shakes my hand.

"I'm so sorry," she says. She's very young, barely out of teacher-training college. "They're just such a handful."

"Don't worry," I say awkwardly, "you'll soon find your feet."

I still feel bad, though, because I know most of my irritation is due to what happened with Marc earlier. After the buses depart, I sit in my office, somewhat dispirited. I had anticipated that he might be angry by my suggestion, but not that it would manifest in the way it had. He hadn't seemed offended; if anything, he'd seemed flattered I'd asked. But I know the way I offered money was wrong. And clearly, he's angry toward Daniel for the way he treated me, and he doesn't know the half of it.

I sigh and get up to sort out the animals. They have a last feed and a fuss before I bed them down for the night, and finally lock up around six thirty. It's been a long day, and I'm tired. Sandra is doing the early shift tomorrow, and will arrive at six a.m., so I think I'll have a couple of glasses of wine and maybe a takeout while I watch a movie, then go to bed early, and have a lie-in tomorrow.

I walk out to my car, then stop in surprise. A ute is parked next to it, and leaning against it is Marc, now dressed in navy suit trousers and a white shirt. Jack sits at his side. My heart gives an uncharacteristic hard bump.

"Hey," he says.

"Hey." I pause in front of him. I feel awkward after what happened earlier, a mixture of resentful and embarrassed. Is he going to yell at me?

But he just says, "Are you hungry? I thought you might like to catch some dinner."

"No, thank you."

"It wouldn't be a date," he says. "I have a business proposition for you." He looks serious, but his eyes sparkle, suggesting he finds something amusing.

"A business proposition?" I repeat.

"Meet me at Between the Sheets," he says, "and I'll tell you all about it."

I hesitate, but I'm starving, and although I don't want to admit it to him, I'm intrigued by his words. Maybe he's decided to help after all. "All right," I say, grudgingly.

"I'll drop Jack off home on the way past," he says.

I walk past him and get in my car. He gets in the ute, and then follows me out and along the road that runs alongside the beach all the way through Paihia, turning off at the end to his road.

I park outside the restaurant, get out, and stand looking out at the Pacific as I wait for him. A family is playing cricket on the beach, two young boys running between pieces of driftwood stuck in the ground for a wicket as Dad cheers them on. For some reason I've always pictured myself with a girl, but of course it could be a boy. My hand strays to my belly, lingering there as I imagine how it must feel to have a life growing inside it. This broodiness—this hunger, and not for food—is new, and it's overwhelming in its intensity.

"Ready?" Marc says. I hadn't heard him pull up. I turn and see him watching me. I nod, and together we walk across the road.

"Restaurant or bar?" he asks.

"Bar," I reply, preferring the relaxed atmosphere. He leads the way into the bar, which is nicely busy. We take a recently vacated table overlooking the beach. The front portion of the building has large doors, and this evening they've been pulled back to let the warm, early evening sea breeze blow across the diners.

We examine the menu and decide to have catch of the day—snapper—and fries, with two beers, and the waiter goes off with our order.

Marc folds his arms and leans on the table, but doesn't say anything for a moment. Instead, he looks into my eyes. His are a dark blue, the color of the sky on the horizon, where rain is coming in. Apparently all babies are born with blue eyes, so if we had one, the baby's eyes would look like his. Mmm.

"So… you said you have a proposition?" I ask him. I have no idea what he's going to come out with.

"I do." Still, he doesn't say what it is.

"What's up?" I ask. "Have you changed your mind?"

"No. I'm thinking about how to phrase it."

Puzzled, I lean back as the waiter returns with our beers. As he walks away, I sip the beer, conscious of Marc's steady stare. "Will you say something?" I prompt. "You're starting to make me nervous."

"Why?"

"You know I can't tell what you're thinking," I reply. "I can never tell what anyone's thinking. I don't know if you're amused or angry."

"I'm neither of those."

"Frustrated?"

"No."

I huff a sigh.

"If I'm anything," he says, "I'm… keyed up."

"Why?"

His lips curve up a little. He has a swig of beer. "Okay," he says eventually. "Let me start by saying I understand why you've made this decision. It's tough when a relationship doesn't work out, and I can see you've been badly hurt, and that you don't want to be hurt again. And I can sympathize with you wanting to have a family. I know that many women make the choice to have a baby when they don't have a partner for various reasons. I admire you for not turning your back on that dream because you don't have a partner."

"Thank you," I say, a little mollified. He's often a one-syllable man, so it's weird to hear him say so much in one go.

"Izzy's been talking a lot about having kids lately," he says. I forget he's her brother sometimes. "She told me how she used to push the thought from her mind when she was single, but now she's with Hal she feels this overwhelming broodiness. So I do understand."

I pick at the label of the beer bottle with my fingernail. "Okay."

"I also understand why you're reluctant to go to a sperm bank, and why you'd rather know the father. And I have to tell you, I'm hugely flattered that you approached me."

I lift my gaze to his. His eyes are warm.

"So…" I draw out the word.

"So… I don't like the idea of you getting pregnant by another man." Keeping his gaze on me as if wanting to see my reaction to that, he swigs from his beer bottle again. I watch his throat constrict as he swallows. He definitely needs a shave.

He puts the bottle down. "I've been thinking about it all afternoon. And I'd like to help you."

Joy fills me. "Really?"

"But…"

My smile fades. "But what?"

"I'm not doing anything in a cup," he states.

I open my mouth to reply, but at that moment the waiter arrives with our food. My heart races, but I make myself sit calmly until the waiter retreats.

Marc puts salt and pepper on his chips, glancing up at me occasionally.

"I don't understand," I say eventually. "So what are you saying?"

He picks up a couple of fries and pops them in his mouth. "I'll help you get pregnant. But I'll only do it the old-fashioned way."

I stare at him as he cuts into his fish, spears a piece on his fork, then dips it in the tartar sauce. He chews it for a moment before lifting his gaze to mine, and then starts laughing at the look on my face.

"You mean…" I'm not sure I can bring myself to say it.

"Yes," he says. "I'm proposing we have sex until I get you pregnant."

My face grows so warm, I know I've turned scarlet. He surveys it with a smile, but he doesn't apologize.

"I don't understand," I tell him again. "My way is easier."

He has a swig of beer. "I think that's arguable."

I'm completely confused now. When I first came up with the idea, I'd hoped he'd say yes because he's my friend, but I presumed one condition would be that he remained anonymous and had no further connection with me, other than our normal friendship and working relationship at the Ark. I'm asking for his help in a way that means he doesn't have to do anything. Hardly anything, except what I'm sure most men do on a regular basis.

"I don't understand what you get out of it," I blurt out.

That makes him laugh. He leans back in his chair for a moment, looking a mixture of puzzled and amused. Then he leans forward again. "You," he said softly. "I get you, Poppy."

"I told you, I don't want a relationship."

"Yes, I know. I'm not offering that; initially, anyway."

"I said I'd pay you," I tell him.

He looks at my plate for a moment. Then he gestures to my fish and chips. "Eat up."

"Marc—"

"Why do you call me Marc and not Fitz?"

I frown. "I thought that was your name?"

"It is."

"Would you rather I called you Fitz?"

"No. I like it. I meant… Oh, never mind. Eat your dinner."

I stare at the fish, then cut up a piece and eat it. It's amazing, probably fresh out of the sea that morning. My head is spinning.

"Let me explain a bit more," he says. "I've been doing some research."

"Into what?"

"Into getting pregnant. I'm sure you probably know most of it, because you've obviously looked into artificial insemination, but it was quite an eye-opener for me. Apparently it's quite common to use what they call a personal donor—a family member or friend. It takes longer if you want to use a clinic-recruited donor because there aren't enough, and single women and same-sex couples have to wait longer."

I nod; I know this.

"They allocate ten inseminations," he continues. "That's for six to seven cycles of IUI or intrauterine insemination, where they place the sperm directly into the uterus, and if that doesn't work, three cycles of IVF, where they add the sperm and egg together outside the body."

"Yes." I'm impressed and touched he's made the effort to find out the details.

"At your age, which is relatively young, the pregnancy rate of IUI is about thirteen percent. And there is a ten to fifteen percent chance of twins. However, the chance of getting pregnant naturally each month is about twenty-five percent."

"True," I admit, "but IVF is higher."

"Yes, you have about a forty-five to fifty percent chance of a birth with each embryo transfer. But there are quite a few risks, and again, possibly a greater chance of a multiple birth depending on how many fertilized eggs they implant."

I concentrate on cutting up my fish. I know he's right.

"Getting pregnant naturally is the safest option," he says. "Plus there are other things we can do to increase the chances of conception."

"Like what?"

His expression turns mischievous. "There is some scientific evidence to suggest an orgasm helps a woman get pregnant."

My eyes widen. "Seriously?"

"Yes. The release of oxytocin decreases stress, which aids getting pregnant, especially if it happens less than a minute before or after the man ejaculates."

I glance around the room to make sure we're not being overheard, hardly able to believe I'm having this conversation over dinner.

Normally I'd have changed the subject well before now, but there's something about Marc's candidness that appeals to me. He's not embarrassed or being crass. He knows I struggle with nuance, and so he's just stating the facts.

Well, they're not facts, because obviously he's got it seriously wrong.

"That's all well and good," I tell him, "but what are the chances of that happening every time a couple has sex?"

He blinks a few times. "You're kidding me, right?"

"What do you mean?"

"I'm confused," he admits.

"Join the club. This conversation is baffling me."

He frowns. "Which bit don't you understand?"

"You said the woman has to have an orgasm less than a minute before or after the guy ejaculates."

"Yeah…" His lips curve up. "I'm not saying it wouldn't need careful timing…"

"Marc, I'm just making the point that it's rare enough that it happens at all, let alone within such a short window."

"For what to happen at all?"

Now I'm exasperated. I lean forward and whisper, somewhat furiously, "For a woman to have an orgasm during sex."

He stares at me. Then he puts down his knife and fork and leans back. "Please tell me you're joking."

"I couldn't be more serious." I'm shocked that he doesn't understand. "You know women fake it, right? Or have you really assumed that every woman you've had sex with has had an orgasm every time?"

Chapter Four

Fitz

I'm not sure I've ever been truly speechless before. I stare at Poppy for so long, she blows out a long breath and swigs her beer.

"I don't know what to say," I admit. "Are you seriously telling me you've never had an orgasm during sex?"

She blushes. "Once or twice. Possibly."

"Jesus Christ."

"That's pretty normal, Marc, believe me."

"No, it really isn't."

She gives a patient sigh, the kind she'd probably use to explain to a ten-year-old that Santa doesn't really exist. "What you see in the movies…" she says gently, "none of that is real. It just doesn't happen that way for women. Not in the real world."

I stab my fork into my fish. "It does with the women I sleep with."

"I'm sorry if it comes as a shock to you, but they were almost certainly faking it."

"No, they weren't."

"How do you know?"

"I just do."

"How?"

I roll my eyes. "I can tell when a woman's enjoying herself."

She looks at me with such doubt that I begin to wonder if she's right. Can I be one hundred percent sure the women I've been with haven't faked it? I suppose I can't. But I've gone to enough effort that I'm pretty certain they haven't needed to.

"So how often do you believe a woman has had an orgasm when she's had sex with you?" she asks, her curiosity overriding her embarrassment.

Am I really discussing this over fish and chips? "Every time," I say. "Well, since I figured out what I was doing, anyway. Since I was about twenty."

She rolls her eyes. "Yeah, right."

"I'm serious," I tell her. "Of course I'm serious. Anything else would be impolite."

She snorts. "Don't make me laugh."

This would be funny if it wasn't so sad. I know there are men, of course, who are clueless about giving a woman pleasure, but I'm sure most of the girls I know wouldn't settle for anything less than a satisfying love life. Why has Poppy?

"How many partners have you had?" I ask her.

She pokes at her fish. "A few."

"And none of them made you come during sex?"

"Like I said, it's quite normal." She obviously doesn't understand my confusion.

"Poppy," I say as gently as I can, looking into her eyes, "it's not."

She stops with a forkful of fish halfway to her mouth. Our gazes lock. I don't smile, making sure she can see I'm serious.

She lowers her fork. "So you're really saying you give a woman an orgasm every time you sleep with her?"

"More than one, usually. And that's something else I found out—apparently if a guy goes down on a woman first, it can increase the amount of semen he produces."

Her jaw drops.

I eat a couple of fries. "I'm just saying. I think it would be more fun than having IVF. And a lot cheaper and less hassle." I sigh. "I can tell by the look on your face you don't believe me."

"I don't. And anyway, you're saying that not only could you give a woman an orgasm every time—*every time*—you had sex, but that you could time it to within a minute of your own climax?" Her voice is heavy with incredulity.

"Give or take. It's not an exact science."

"Jesus, Marc. How on earth would you do that?"

Now it's my turn to laugh. "Sleep with me and you'll find out."

Both of us eat our fries, studying each other.

"You really are serious about this," she says eventually.

"I am."

"Because you want to have sex with me."

"No. Well, yes, obviously—I mean not only because I want to have sex with you. I'm saying give me one month to try to get you pregnant the traditional way. We'll have sex as often as I can manage it, and I'll do my best to carry out the other suggestions to increase the likelihood of it happening. And hopefully, at the end of the month, you'll be pregnant, and you'll have fallen so madly in love with all those orgasms I'm going to give you that we'll end up getting married, grow old and gray, and play Scrabble in the retirement village together with our teeth in a glass." I smile.

She doesn't. "You want to try to seduce me into a relationship," she says.

I don't see any sense in lying. "Yes."

"It won't work," she advises softly.

"We'll see."

"I won't fall for you," she states. "I won't let myself."

I get the first twinge of warning that I could be putting myself in the path of a potential disaster. But it's too late now. "What have you got to lose? Hopefully you'll get pregnant if nothing else."

"And if I do? Are you going to want to see the baby? Tell everyone it's yours?"

"I'd like to. But I swear to you, if you get pregnant, and after a month with me you tell me then that you don't want me involved, I'll back away, and I won't cause trouble for you. Cross my heart."

She pokes at her fish with her fork.

"Come on," I tease. "Do you really want to get pregnant by a doctor sticking a syringe inside you? I'm no scientist, but it must make a difference if a baby is conceived with affection. And I have a lot of affection for you. We're good friends, aren't we?"

She studies my face, her green eyes thoughtful. "Yes," she says eventually. "We are."

"Well, then. What's stopping you?"

"I don't want to break your heart."

That makes my eyebrows rise. "Why don't you let me worry about that?"

She finishes off her fish and sits back. I can see something else is bothering her.

"Out with it," I tell her.

"As you said, we're good friends and… I like you. I don't want to disappoint you."

"In what way?"

"In bed."

"Why on earth would you disappoint me in…" My voice trails off. She's talking about Daniel. The bastard criticized her about sex. Holy fucking shit, I'm going to smash the son of a bitch's face in.

"Right," I tell her, "that's it. We're definitely having sex. And lots of it, until I can convince you how amazing you are."

That makes her laugh. The waiter comes over and takes our plates, then asks us if we want a dessert.

"They do a mean chocolate sundae here," I advise Poppy. She nods, so I ask for two sundaes, and the waiter goes off again.

She looks out across the beach, lost in thought, so I take the opportunity to study her. The late evening sun gives her pale skin an amber glow and turns her hair to a flaming red. I can imagine how it would look spread out across a white pillow. My heart aches for her. I'm no Casanova, but even with my rudimentary skills in the bedroom, I like to think I can give a woman a good time. I want to take Poppy to bed and watch her face light up as she realizes how wrong Daniel was. I want to prove to her she's a goddess, and the only thing she has to do to turn me on is to be there.

I know she's withdrawn socially since her breakup. Nix told me she rarely goes out with the other girls, and at work she tends to keep to herself over at the petting farm. Her breakup severely traumatized her. I want to mend that wound. Even if we don't work out, if I can make her feel better about herself, and about having a relationship, it'll be worth it.

She's obviously thinking about what I've said, because she stays lost in thought until the waiter returns with our sundaes.

I dip my spoon in the chocolate ice cream and have a spoonful. Poppy does the same, scooping up some whipped cream and tiny marshmallows with it, and sighing as she places it in her mouth. "Mmm. That's lovely." She turns her spoon over and sucks the ice cream off it, watching me curiously.

"You're thinking about all those orgasms, aren't you?" I ask her, delving the spoon into the chocolate sauce.

"I still think you're fibbing," she says. "I don't believe any man would bother to bring a woman to a climax every time they have sex."

"That's where you're wrong. Many men enjoy foreplay, and anyway, the decent ones want to please their girl and make sure they enjoy it.

It's also another point for the sex versus IVF debate. Studies suggest that taking time to arouse a woman increases sperm count. And there's evidence that the lubrication a woman produces during foreplay creates an ideal environment for sperm to swim and survive. There's scientific proof that nature wants you to have good sex."

"Even if that was true," she says, "it doesn't mean it happens on a regular basis. Most guys aren't patient at the best of times."

"Jesus, Poppy, you're talking as if it takes three hours."

"Well…"

I reach out my spoon and steal a Malteser from the top of her sundae. She notices, but doesn't say anything. "Let's put it this way," I say. "How long does it take you to achieve an orgasm when you're on your own?"

That shocks her. She stares at me, her mouth open, and a touch of color appears in her cheeks. "I… um…"

She seemed to like me being open, but maybe I was a little frank there. "My point is," I add a bit more gently, "I'm guessing it's not three hours. Ten, twenty minutes? Sometimes less, sometimes more? If you communicate what you like and what turns you on, why should it be any different with the man in your life?"

Even as I say it, one word jumps out at me. Communicate. The very thing she struggles with. Maybe Daniel, and the other guys she's been with, never asked her what she liked. Or maybe they did and she couldn't bring herself to tell them, or perhaps she doesn't even know how to put it into words. I've always assumed that all modern women are confident and knowledgeable about their bodies—certainly the ones I've been with have been. But of course not everyone is going to be like that. I read a survey a few years ago that stated over eighty percent of men and over sixty percent of women were unable to identify the vagina on a medical illustration of the female reproductive tract. I don't think Poppy is quite that bad, but it's clear that not everyone is au fait with every element of sex.

"So okay," I tell her, my heart aching for her, "as well as getting you pregnant, this is going to be an adventure. A training session, if you will. We're good friends, and we can talk, can't we? You'll be able to explain to me what you like, and I'll be able to show you how enjoyable sex can be when it's done right."

She sucks more ice cream off her spoon. "You're very sure of yourself."

"It's not rocket science, that's all. Don't you ever talk to the other girls about sex? Nix and Remy and Izzy?"

She shakes her head.

"You should. I'm sure they'd put you straight."

She scrapes at the bottom of her glass. "You were right. This is a very good sundae."

I give in, knowing she's not going to believe anything I say until she can verify it for herself. "You'll think about it, anyway?"

She nods and pushes her glass away. "I will." She swigs the last of her beer and wipes her mouth, watching me finishing my sundae. I offer her the last Malteser on my spoon. She studies it somewhat wryly, meets my eyes, then leans forward and takes it off the spoon. I try not to think of other places her lips might close around, and give a silent sigh.

"Thank you," she says. I'm not sure if she's thanking me for the Malteser or our talk.

"You're welcome."

"I appreciate you trying to help me, even if it is in a different way from what I was planning."

"I do want to help, I swear."

"Yes. Because your offer is purely altruistic."

"Of course it isn't. I'll thoroughly enjoy impregnating you."

We both laugh and get to our feet, pay the bill, then head back to our cars. We pause by hers, looking down the beach, where the kids who were playing cricket are now jumping about in the waves.

"Do you want a boy or a girl?" I ask her.

"Don't tell me… You've discovered a way to choose the sex of your baby by using a particular position."

That makes me laugh, and she joins in, nudging me with her elbow.

"I'll see you at work tomorrow?" I ask. When she nods, I bend and kiss her cheek. "Have a good evening."

I get in my car, watching her get in hers, then follow her down the road until I turn off for my apartment. She gives me a wave, then continues along the road to Opua, where she has a big house on a hill overlooking the bay. I'm not poor by any means, but I don't have anywhere near the kind of money the Kings have.

I'm glad that Izzy is married to Hal now. She'll never want for anything, money or love. But it shows you how money doesn't buy everything. Poppy has more money than she could ever spend, but it really can't buy you love.

Chapter Five

Poppy

I rock the baby boy in my arms, tenderness filling me at the sight of his button nose, his long lashes, and his flushed cheeks.

"He's so gorgeous," I tell his mother, Abby. "You're so lucky."

"I know. He takes after Noah."

She smiles, and I smile back. It's such a lovely thing to say. Ethan is Noah's baby in every way except blood. He even delivered him. I still can't believe that. I'd have been frightened witless if a friend went into labor, but even though Noah's wife had died in childbirth, along with the baby, Noah stayed by Abby's side until the baby was born.

They're getting married at Christmas. Noah's agoraphobia has been so much better that he's said he's going to fly everyone somewhere exotic for the wedding.

"Any idea where the wedding is going to be, yet?" I ask Abby.

She shakes her head. "We're still thinking about it. I worry a little that when it's time to get on the plane, he's going to freeze, but he seems confident he'll be okay, and he's certainly been better lately."

"You've been good for him," I tell her. "He's so happy right now."

"Aw." She stretches out her legs and sips her tea. "Yeah, I have to admit, life could be a lot worse."

We're in the conservatory at Noah's house, looking out over the Bay of Islands. It's a bright, blustery spring day, and their two German Shepherds are lying on the deck, enjoying the warm breeze.

I've been coming over a lot since Abby had the baby. I love seeing Ethan, and Abby and I have struck up a friendship, which I'm enjoying. I don't make friends easily, and I suspect she doesn't either, so it's nice for the two of us to have someone to chat to.

Noah's working in his office, and Abby has been baking this morning, filling the house with the mouthwatering aroma of sponge cakes. She's been posting recordings of herself decorating fancy cakes on YouTube, and she already has tons of followers. We're having a slice of one of the cakes now with our coffee—a jam-and-cream-filled sponge topped with Disney characters made from fondant icing. She definitely has a talent for it.

"Have you got something on your mind?" Abby asks. "You seem distracted."

I don't answer for a moment, smiling at Ethan, who has opened his eyes and is looking up at me. He grabs my finger and tries to put it in his mouth and suck it. I laugh and kiss his head.

"Sort of," I reply finally. I've been trying to pluck up the courage to talk to Abby about this. I can't think of anyone else to talk to. My mother would always help me if she could, but this isn't the type of thing you talk to your mom about. Izzy would have been another option, but she's in Fiji on her honeymoon with Hal. Nix and Remy are both younger than me, and although they're both very open, I don't feel comfortable talking about this with them. My sister is the other option, but although Summer and I are close, I kinda don't want to admit to her that I have a problem in this area.

"I wondered whether I could ask you a personal question," I begin.

"Of course." Abby accepts Ethan from me as he starts to grizzle, puts him to the breast, then smiles at me. "Fire away."

"It's a little embarrassing." I study my hands. "It's about sex."

"Oh, okay! Well, I'm hardly the expert." She laughs. "Although if Noah has anything to do with it, I will be soon."

That makes me chuckle. I love the fact that Noah's finally getting some after so many years of solitude. "That's good to hear." I curl up in the chair and warm my hands on my mug of coffee. "The thing is… I've been talking to someone… a guy… and he said something I didn't believe, but he got me wondering… and I feel I need to ask someone else to find out, because it's not really the kind of thing you can Google and be sure you're getting the right answer, you know?"

"Sort of. I do know that I found it very helpful when Summer was so open with me. I've never really had the kind of friends you could talk to about sex, but she made it seem very normal to be able to discuss everything."

"Yes," I agree, "she's very down to earth."

"So what did this guy say to you?" Abby asks. She doesn't press me to find out who he is yet.

I take a deep breath. "He seemed to think it was very normal for a woman to achieve an orgasm every time she went to bed with him. I told him she would have been faking it, because I couldn't believe any guy would bother to bring a woman to climax every time they had sex. But this guy was adamant he was right and I was wrong. I haven't had that much experience, just four guys over the years, but none of them have ever been interested in foreplay, and I've hardly ever climaxed during sex. And I just wondered what you thought."

My face has grown warm. Part of me was worried Abby might laugh, but she frowns thoughtfully.

"I haven't had that much experience," she says. "I was with Tom for fourteen years, and before him there were only two other guys, and we were very young, so there wasn't a lot of foreplay going on."

"And with Tom?"

She hesitates, concentrating on making sure Ethan's getting his milk. I'm sure she feels awkward talking about her ex, and I half wish I hadn't brought the topic up.

But she looks up, and I can see she's been thinking about what to say. "I read an article in a women's magazine once," she says. "It said twenty percent of women seldom have an orgasm, and five percent never have one. I certainly don't think your experience is isolated. It also said something like seventy-five percent can't reach orgasm from intercourse alone, and that was certainly my experience. When Tom and I were younger, and we spent a lot of time in bed, things were better, but as the years went by and sex became more perfunctory, he became less concerned with my pleasure, and in the end it was just about him achieving a climax. If I wanted one, I had to organize it myself." She gives me an amused look.

I feel some relief at her words—that I'm not alone. "But now?" I ask. "With Noah? Sorry, I don't mean to pry, but..." I can't explain how important it is for me to understand.

Her smile turns mischievous. "Oh, things are a lot better with Noah. He's very unselfish. Maybe it's because he's older, and has been alone for a long time. I don't know. I mean, men aren't born knowing how to pleasure a woman. We're complicated creatures and it takes time. They have to want to do it."

"But in your experience, some men do?"

"Oh yes." She sighs and shifts Ethan to the other breast. "You sound very like me. I never talked about this, either. And then I met

Summer, and Nix, and Remy, who are all very open about their love lives, and it was like a revelation. They obviously all have a fulfilling sex life. You can tell from what they say. I think a lot of it depends on the guy, and your relationship with him. If he loves you, and he's kind and generous, and you're able to talk, there's no reason it won't be amazing."

I chew my bottom lip. Marc doesn't love me, but he is kind and generous. So it's possible that he was telling the truth? Every time he has sex with a woman, he's able to give her an orgasm?

Oh.

My.

God.

"So…" Abby draws out the word. "Are you going to tell me who this mystery man is?"

"Um…" We both smile, then start laughing. "It's not a thing," I say. "We're not dating or anything."

"But you're obviously thinking about it."

"It's complicated."

"Isn't it always?"

I sigh. "It's Marc."

She looks confused. "Marc who?"

"Fitzgerald."

"Oh, Fitz!" She laughs. "I didn't know that was his first name." Her eyes dance. "I see. I'd heard he was interested in you."

"He asked me out the night of the cyclone."

"Oh, and?"

"I said no. I don't want another relationship."

I wait for her to argue with me, but her expression just softens, and she says, "I understand. So… why the questions about orgasms, then?"

I give in and explain it all to her. That I approached him to be a sperm donor, and he told me he'll only get me pregnant the old-fashioned way.

She stares at me, trying hard not to laugh, then gives in and giggles. "What a naughty boy."

I roll my eyes. "Tell me about it."

"What did you say?"

"That I'd think about it. I don't know what to do. I've told him I'm not interested in a relationship, but he admitted he's hoping that after we've slept together it'll change everything."

SERENITY WOODS

"It might," she points out.

"It won't," I reply. "I won't let it. But he thinks it will, and it seems unfair to keep him hanging on, hoping."

"You told him this?"

"Yes, of course."

"What did he say?"

"That it was his problem and I should let him worry about it."

"He has a point."

"So you think I should go for it?"

Her lips curve up. "Let's go over it again. He's agreed to help you get pregnant. You won't have to go to a hospital, you won't have to see a doctor, you can maximize the chance of the sperm meeting the egg by having sex multiple times, and on top of it he's offered you boundless wonderful orgasms."

"Well if you put it like that…"

We both dissolve into laughter, and we're both still giggling when Noah appears at the door.

"Something funny?" he says, amused.

"No," I say immediately, giving Abby a warning glance. She mimes zipping her mouth closed, and I laugh. "We're just comparing notes."

"And it made you laugh? That doesn't sound promising."

"Aw." I stand and kiss his cheek. "Let's just say you came out of it very positively, Noah King."

I say goodbye to Abby and thank her for her help. Ethan has fallen asleep, and I bend and kiss his forehead before going with Noah to the front door.

"Everything all right?" he asks as he opens it.

I study his face. He was nearly fourteen when I was born, and he'd already met and married Lisa by the time I was in my teens. I can still remember the day Lisa died, and how I'd gone with Mom and Dad to his house in Auckland and watched Dad hug him, my heart breaking as he'd cried into Dad's shoulder. He'd loved Lisa so much, and yet here he was, loving again. The heart has an amazing capacity to heal and regenerate.

Is it possible it's in the stars for me to love again?

I push the notion away. I'm not even going there. Opening oneself up to the possibility of love means accepting there's a chance of being hurt, and I'm not ready for that. I don't know if I ever will be.

"I'm fine," I tell Noah. "Your lady is a lovely woman."

He chuckles. "Yes, she is."

"And your baby is gorgeous."

"He is. You need to get yourself one of those, Poppy. You'd make a lovely mom."

I blink with some surprise, touched by his words. Nobody's ever said that to me before.

He smiles. "Have a great day."

"Yes, see you." I walk out into the sunshine, my hair lifting in the breeze. His words stay with me as I walk back along the path to the Ark. What a lovely thing to say.

I worry a lot about my ability to connect with people, especially after the things Daniel said. I know others see me as odd. When I've been with my mother and Summer in waiting rooms and in bus queues, people just start talking to them—they always seem to find something to talk about. But there's something about me that makes others hold back. If I'm in a waiting room, people will fill all the other seats before they take the one next to me. I guess I must give out signals, although I'm not aware of them. Or maybe I am. I hope someone doesn't sit next to me because then I would have to make up something to talk about. I prefer being on my own. And then I feel lonely.

I stop and lean on the fence, overlooking the field where a couple of horses graze contentedly. I'm hoping having a child will fill that hole inside me. I don't want the complications of a relationship, of worrying about pleasing someone else and fearing I've said the wrong thing, but I do need love and fulfilment, and I hope a child will provide that.

Is it selfish to want a baby and deny it the presence of a father? Fifty years ago, a huge stigma was attached to single parents, and I'd have been the talk of the town, but it's no longer like that. There are so many single moms and dads, and lots of people going to sperm banks because they want the same as I do—a child without the complication of a partner. I don't think I'm unusual. And anyway, what does it matter? I've been thinking about it for a long, long time, and the decision feels right.

And now I have this chance. And it involves no doctor's appointments, no hormonal drugs or injections or syringes. And it wouldn't be cold and clinical. Is Marc right? Does it make a difference whether a baby is conceived with affection? Hmm, obviously it's not correct or else every baby born through IVF and especially any adopted child would have a bad relationship with their parents, and that's certainly not the case in my family.

And yet something deep inside me wants to believe it.

Or is it just that I'm enticed by the multitude of orgasms he's promising me? I purse my lips.

But no, it's more than that. After thinking that other people see me as odd, I'm touched that he's attracted to me. That he's bothered to spend time talking to me this year. And that he doesn't seem put off by my weirdness. I'm going to have to make sure I take steps to ensure it's a temporary thing, that's all, and I think I know the best way to do that.

So am I going to go for it? I suck my bottom lip, feeling a swell of excitement, and place my hand on my belly. This time next month, I could be pregnant.

The draw of multiple orgasms is just an added bonus…

Chapter Six

Fitz

"I think you should take the plans for the new building," Leon says. "I know Noah emailed them, but you know those big paper ones we wrote all over—there are some really useful notes on there."

I nod and make a mental note to get them off Noah. On Sunday, I'm flying down to Hawke's Bay to spend a few days with the estate manager of the new Ark, to talk about what's worked and hasn't worked over here in the bay and check things out first-hand for Noah. He's talked about going down there himself, but even though he's improving every day, I don't think he's quite up to flying yet.

We're standing in the square, out the front of the Ark. Jack's playing with Ziggy, one of Leon's Dalmatians. Even though we've got a meeting later on in the day to discuss finances, we often end up talking out here when we bump into each other on the way to or from the break room.

"I thought about calling in at that garden center not far from the new Ark," I tell Leon, "so I can show Ashton what kind of trees we've got surrounding the…" My voice trails off as I see Poppy come around the veterinary center and enter the square. She's obviously coming back from Noah's house. I know she goes up there quite often to see Abby and Ethan.

Leon studies me, then follows my gaze. "Hey," he says to Poppy, who falters as she sees us, then crosses the square at Leon's welcome.

"Morning." She stops before us, glances at me, then smiles at Leon before bending to fuss the dogs.

Man, she looks amazing today. Her curly hair, which she often wears tied back, is loose this morning, and it's wild in the breeze and glowing in the sunlight. She's wearing tight jeans and a bright blue sweater that makes her look like a spring flower. She's gorgeous.

"Been up to see Noah?" Leon asks.

She nods and smiles. "And cuddle Ethan, of course."

Leon looks at me, then back at her and clears his throat. "Well, I'd better go. Have a good morning." He catches my eye and winks. I scowl at him, and he gives a short laugh and goes into the office building, Ziggy at his heels.

I turn my attention to Poppy, who's looking up at me with her huge green eyes. Considering she's a King, she's not particularly tall, maybe five-six or seven. She's slender and small-boned. I think she'd feel tiny in my arms.

"Morning," I say to her.

"Good morning."

"Did you have a nice time with Abby and Ethan?"

"I did." She lowers her gaze to her feet and studies them. "I had a chat to her. I hope that was okay."

My eyebrows rise. "What about?"

"About our... possible arrangement."

"Oh?" It interests me that she's vocalized it to a friend. "You told her you wanted a baby?"

"Yes... although we talked more about... you know..." She blushes.

My lips curve up. "And? What did she say?"

"She confirmed that my experience isn't unusual." She lifts her gaze to me.

I frown. "Really?"

"Mm. But she also suggested there are men out there who are more considerate than those I've had the misfortune to pair up with."

"I'm glad to hear it." I thank Abby in my head. And Noah, bless him.

Poppy clears her throat. "So... I've been giving it some thought, and I think I've decided to take you up on your offer."

Our gazes lock, and a tingle runs through me from the top of my head to the tips of my toes.

"Wow," I say softly. "You've made my day."

She smiles. "That's a nice thing to say."

I slide my gaze to her lips. "I wish I could kiss you."

Now her look turns wry. "In the middle of the square? I don't think so. And I feel it makes sense at this moment to point out again that this is a temporary arrangement with one main purpose—to get me pregnant."

"Understood."

"Marc…"

"I get it," I protest. "And I'm happy to comply."

"With this in mind, I want to reiterate that I would pay you for your services."

I stare at my shoes for a moment.

"I'd be saving money because I wouldn't be having IVF," she explains. "It's only fair that you get something out of it. And I also think it would be a good idea to keep it in our minds that it's a business transaction, and nothing more."

I need the money. I want to have sex with her. I want to help her. So there's no reason I should say no.

The acceptance sticks to my lips, though. Am I really reduced to earning money by being paid to have sex? *There's a word for that, Fitz…* But I remind myself she doesn't mean it like that. Albie would say she's trying to protect herself. She certainly doesn't mean to insult me, I know that.

"All right," I say, although I feel a twinge of regret. I push it away. It'll be worth it.

Poppy glances around, presumably making sure nobody's watching us. "I think it's best if we keep our relationship to ourselves."

"Fair enough. So… I'm excited to get started," I tell her. I look at my watch. "What are you up to now?"

She gives a short laugh and nudges me. "Is this what I can expect over the next few weeks?"

"It's exactly what you can expect. We want to optimize your chances, don't we?"

She brushes her hair back from her face. "Sex two days before ovulation, and on the day of ovulation, increases the chance of getting pregnant to around thirty percent."

"Do you know when you're ovulating?"

She nods. "It's around day fourteen of my cycle. That's around next Tuesday."

I open my mouth to say that it makes sense to get going immediately, then realize what's happening next week. "Shit."

"What?"

"I'm away from Sunday for the week. I'm going to Hawke's Bay for Noah to check out the new Ark."

"Oh. Well. Never mind. There's always next month."

I study her face, hating the fact that her smile has slipped. She's agreed to try to get pregnant by sleeping together. She's agreed to sleep with me. No way am I going to let this opportunity pass.

"I have an idea," I tell her.

"Oh?"

"Come to Hawke's Bay with me."

She stares at me. "Seriously?"

"Yeah. You can come and look around the new Ark, maybe chat to the manager about the petting farm. And we can spend some time alone, too. It means we wouldn't have to creep around like we'd have to up here." The more I talk about it, the more I think it's a brilliant idea.

"But... I'm working..."

"Have you had a vacation at all this year?" Her expression tells me she hasn't. "Sandra will be happy to cover for you, I'm sure. And all that rest and relaxation... and sex... would be conducive for getting pregnant..." I smile.

She chews her bottom lip. "Where would we stay?"

"Why don't you leave that to me? I'll find us somewhere nice. Just the two of us. For a week." I get all hot and bothered at the thought. "So, thirty percent eh?"

"Mm. Thirty percent."

"There's a good chance you could have a small bump by Christmas."

Her eyes widen, and then she gives me the most beautiful smile. "I suppose."

"I'll do my best," I tell her.

"I'm sure you will."

Our gazes lock again, and heat rushes through me at the thought that it's only going to be a couple of days until I have her in my bed. Until I can do all the things I've been dreaming of doing to her and with her since we met.

I gloss over the fact that it's supposed to be temporary. One step at a time. It might take her longer than a few months to get pregnant. We'd just have to keep on trying, wouldn't we?

"Leave it all with me," I tell her. "I'll talk to Noah and make sure he's okay with you taking time off, and then I'll get everything booked."

"Okay," she says softly, "I'd better get back to work."

"Have a great day."

"You too." She drops her gaze and walks away, twisting her hair into a spiral over her shoulder as the wind tries to fly it like a kite.

I watch her for a minute or two, then turn and go into my office. I sit in my chair for a long while, looking out of the window. Then I decide it's pointless to mull over it, and it makes more sense to get everything done.

First things first. I pick up the phone and dial Noah's mobile.

He answers within a couple of rings. "Noah King."

"Noah, it's Fitz."

"Hey, Fitz. How're you doing?"

"Yeah, good thanks. I have something to run by you. Would you mind if Poppy took next week off?"

"Poppy?"

"She's not had a vacation all year, and I thought she could do with a break."

"She doesn't have to ask me, Fitz. She's her own boss."

"Yeah, but we like to run things past you, make sure you don't have any brilliant schemes planned or anything."

He laughs. "No, I don't."

"In that case... I was thinking of taking her with me to Hawke's Bay."

"Oh..." He chuckles. "I see."

"Don't start."

"I have to admit, Abby told me a little about what she and Poppy were discussing."

"Jesus." I roll my eyes. "Nothing's private in this place."

"Damn straight. Can't help if I don't know about it."

"I don't need any help, thanks."

"Yeah, that's what I said, and look what happened to me."

That makes me laugh. Last month, his friends and family engineered a night together for him and Abby. He complained, but it was clear to all of us they both needed a gentle push.

"So... she wants a baby, hmm?" Noah says.

"Uh, yeah. I'm flattered she asked me. She won't go out with me, so I told her I'd help her out if we got to… you know, spend some time together."

"Very astute." I can tell he's smiling. "I hope it works out for you."

"Anyway… just wanted to check it was okay for Poppy to take time off and go with me. I'll pay for her flight, obviously." Shit—I'd forgotten about that, but I can't ask the Ark to fund our fling.

"Pay? Aren't you taking the Yonder Star?" He's referring to the plane that belongs to the King family, a reference to Brock, Charlie, and Matt King's business, the Three Wise Men.

"No."

"Why not?"

"I'm not a King, Noah. The rest of us minions fly economy class."

"Jesus," he says, "I'm not a real King, if you're going to be pedantic about it. I'm not blood-related to Matt, remember?"

"I had forgotten, but that's hardly the point."

"It's completely the point. You're as much a part of the family as I am. Take the plane—let the girl travel in style."

I smile. "All right."

"She'll enjoy seeing the new Ark," Noah says. "And there are a couple of petting farms down there—she might like to get some ideas. You know, in between all the baby-making."

"I'm going now."

He laughs. "And I'm also transferring some money across as expenses for a hotel."

"You don't need to do that—"

"It's done." I hear him clicking his mouse. "Can't have our employees roughing it. Choose somewhere nice."

I sigh. "All right. Thank you."

"No worries. Have a great day." He hangs up.

I blow out a breath. So now Albie, Noah, and Abby know what's going on. Poppy's plan to keep it a secret isn't going to last long at this rate.

I think about Noah's words, *You're as much a part of the family as I am.* It's not true, of course; I haven't inherited the vast sums of money the others have. In fact, I'm probably the poorest one at the Ark now that Izzy's married Hal. Stefan's mom is a world-class computer engineer so he's loaded, and everyone else has inherited the family fortune.

But it was a nice thing for Noah to say. The guy really does want to save the world with his Ark, and he's done a pretty good job so far, with Hal, Leon, and Albie finding their perfect partner here, as well as himself.

My thoughts linger on Poppy, and my lips curve up. For the first time, I have a chance to win her. No wonder Noah wants to help.

I turn to my computer and start searching for places to stay. I want to find somewhere magical and romantic, somewhere special…

My gaze falls on a small cottage next to a windmill. That would be cool. It's incredibly short notice, though, and when I click on the calendar, it's grayed out.

I pick up my phone, ring the owner, and double check it's definitely booked. "Unfortunately, yes," she says, to my disappointment. "But we have just had a cancellation on one of our other properties. It's a beauty, too, very quiet and special." She gives me the website address and I click on it. My jaw drops.

"It's perfect," I tell her, my heart racing. Oh, I can't wait to see Poppy's face when we arrive.

I give the woman my name, address, and credit card details, then hang up and sit back, studying the screen with a smug smile. A whole week with Poppy to myself in this amazing place. This is what dreams are made of.

And now I really should get some work done. I give Jack some fuss, then, somewhat reluctantly, I pull a pile of invoices toward me and start signing.

I leave the accommodation on the screen, though, and glance at it occasionally through the rest of the day, a smile on my face.

Chapter Seven

Poppy

On Sunday, the Yonder Star takes off mid-afternoon, heading for the region of Hawke's Bay on the east coast.

"Who's looking after Jack?" I ask Marc. "You two are usually inseparable. It's odd to see you without him."

"Yeah, I miss him," he says. "But I'm trading him in for more interesting company." He smiles. "Ryan's got him this week. He'll spoil him rotten. He'll probably be ten pounds heavier by the time I get back."

"Ryan or Jack?"

He laughs. He has very nice teeth. It's not normally something I would comment on, but he has a lovely smile, when it does appear. Today he's wearing a casual navy shirt, open at the neck, hanging loose over black jeans. He looks equally good in this as he does in a suit or in coveralls. He's had a shave, too, although his hair is still a little long.

I can't believe I'm escaping with him for a whole week. We're going to have sex. Holy moly.

"Have you been to Hawke's Bay before?" Marc asks me.

"I haven't," I admit. "I've been to the Bay of Plenty and Wellington, but for some reason never got to Hawke's Bay. How about you?"

He pauses as Chris, our flight attendant, brings us over a latte each and a plate of club sandwiches.

"Mmm, thank you," I tell him. I love flying on the Yonder Star. I flew quite a bit in economy class when I was younger, which is almost always a trial, especially on long haul. There's nothing like being on your own private plane. I appreciate the luxury of the peace and the space.

"You're welcome." Chris smiles and retreats behind the curtain at the end of the cabin, leaving us alone.

Marc chooses a sandwich and then looks out of the window. I get the feeling he's thinking about what to say. I eat my sandwich while I wait, but he's lost in thought for a long time, and eventually I say, "You okay?"

He brings his attention back to me. "Sorry. I was thinking." He has a bite of his sandwich. "I'm not used to talking about myself."

"I know what you mean. Me neither."

He puts the sandwich down and leans on the table. "I haven't told anyone about my time in Hawke's Bay. Only Izzy knows."

"Oh. Okay." I'm flattered that he wants to confide in me, but puzzled that he apparently has a secret. "I won't tell anyone. Especially Albie, if you don't want the whole Ark to find out."

He studies his drink for a moment. "I used to live in Napier. I moved there for a while toward the end of my Army days."

"Did you have to do training there or something?"

"No." He sighs. "It was because of a woman."

For some reason, I'm surprised. I don't know why. Did I really think he'd get to his early thirties and not have met someone special? I feel a pang of something and analyze it for a moment. Oh. I think it's jealousy. How strange. It's not an emotion I've encountered much in my life. Even when I was with Daniel, I rarely felt jealous, even when I saw him with female teachers at school.

Maybe it's not jealousy, maybe it's more envy. I'm envious that another woman was close to him. And yet it obviously didn't work out.

He's watching me as if gauging my reaction, although I'm sure my feelings aren't playing on my face like a movie screen. Daniel always said he couldn't tell what I was thinking.

Marc clears his throat. "I was very nearly married."

My eyebrows rise. "Really?"

He nods. "Her name was Carmella, but she was known as Mel. She was the sister of a mate of mine. I was in the Army when I met her. We dated whenever I came home on leave, and about seven years ago now, I asked her to marry me. She said yes, and we moved in together and started planning the wedding. And then I had the accident."

He looks out of the window. "They flew me home, and I was in hospital for a while, then in therapy. I fractured my pelvis and damaged a couple of vertebrae. I had to have titanium plates screwed in. I had to learn to walk again."

I'm shocked. "Oh Marc, I didn't know." No wonder he has a limp and an achy back. He walks amazingly well considering.

"It was a tough time. Looking back, I think I was so tied up in my own problems I didn't realize we were growing apart. A week before the wedding, she rang to tell me she was calling it off."

My jaw drops. "Oh no."

"She kept saying she was sorry, but she couldn't give me a reason why; she just said she'd changed her mind. I was absolutely stunned. I'd had no idea she was unhappy."

We sit quietly for a moment as I process what he's told me. The story explains a lot about him. Why he's so quiet, and keeps to himself. Why so many people think he's grouchy.

"Was she seeing someone else?" I wonder.

He shrugs. "Never found out. I suspect so, as she married someone else within a year. Either she'd met him while I was on Scott Base, or maybe she didn't like the idea of being married to a man who was less than whole." His lips twist.

"You're hardly less than whole," I scold. "If I didn't know about your accident, it would be difficult to tell there was anything wrong. Lots of people have backache."

"I didn't mean that," he says. "I meant mentally."

"What do you mean?"

"The accident changed me. I was happy-go-lucky before. Life and soul of the party, you know? I did a lot of sports—rugby, soccer, cricket, hockey. I was super fit. After the accident, I couldn't do any of that. It was an effort just to walk. I felt resentful and angry. I had bouts of depression. I guess I wasn't the person she fell in love with."

"But when you love someone, you should support them in a crisis like that," I protest.

He gives me the ghost of a smile. "That's a nice thing to say, but I know I was hard work. Still am. You were probably right to say no to dating me. I don't mean that to sound self-pitying, but everyone's right when they call me grumpy and a grouch. I know I am. I'm not easy to live with. Even I struggle with myself sometimes."

"That's not why I said no," I tell him softly. I feel a twinge of guilt at turning him down. That can't have helped his ego. "My reasons were purely personal; nothing to do with you. I like you, Marc. I think any woman would be lucky to have a man like you." I mean it. I know the others at the Ark think he's monosyllabic and cantankerous, but he's never like that with me. He's always trying to get me to talk, always teasing. "I don't care what you were like back then," I tell him. "But I like you the way you are now."

"That's only because you didn't know me back then," he points out.

"Maybe. The point is, I think you're perfectly lovely."

That makes him chuckle. "Well, thank you."

"So have you dated much since then?" I'm curious. I haven't seen him with any women at the Ark.

He shakes his head. "I went on a couple of dates with a girl last year, but that's about it."

"Why didn't you see her again?"

He shrugs. "She was nice enough, but there was no spark. She was very... talkative. Which isn't a problem in itself as it's nice to keep the conversation going, but ever since the accident..."

"You treasure your solitude."

"I do. Partly because I also had a whack on the back of the head and a concussion, and I find since then it takes me longer than it did to process things. Loud noises, too many voices, too much conversation... It makes my head hurt."

"I'm glad you told me," I say. "I won't be offended if you tell me to shut up."

He smiles. "Oh I don't get it with you at all. You're very softly spoken, and you don't chatter on about nothing. When you talk, it's always because you have something to say. I like that." His gaze caresses me gently.

The truth is, I like his quiet manner, too. I find him restful. Many of the other guys I know are very 'in your face'—Albie can be a sweetheart but he's always joking around; Hal's larger than life and has a witty answer to everything; Leon shouts a lot—I have no idea how Nix puts up with him. It's nice to be with someone who also prefers the quiet life.

"You said you partly treasure your solitude because of your concussion," I say. "Is there another reason?"

"Just that the accident changed how I feel about things. I don't enjoy... frivolity the way I used to." He frowns.

"I would imagine a brush with death can send a person either way," I tell him gently. "It could make you more outgoing, with an urge to squeeze every last drop out of life. Or it could make you more mindful, with a desire to appreciate each moment, especially in nature."

I've seen him take long walks with Jack over the clifftop. I presumed it was for exercise for them both, but now I think maybe it was as respite for his soul, too. There are few places more beautiful in the world than the Bay of Islands. I can think of worse parts of the world in which to heal.

His gaze lingers on me. "There aren't many people who understand. I'm glad you do."

I choose another sandwich to hide my bashfulness. "So tell me about the Army. Were you posted to places other than Scott Base?"

He brightens a little. He obviously enjoyed his time in the New Zealand Defence Force. "Afghanistan and Iraq. I was an officer, in Training and Development."

"You liked your job."

"I did. I enjoyed the lifestyle. It's good for a young guy—lots of exercise, activities, travel, a great social life."

"You couldn't have stayed in after your accident? Taken a desk job?"

"I could have, but I couldn't bear it—the pity, the sympathy. I needed to get away from it all. Do something completely different."

"What got you into working at the Ark?"

"Izzy, Hal, and Stefan had graduated from veterinary college the year before, and were in the process of setting up the Ark with Noah. I've known the guys for years—most of us went to the same school, and I kept in touch with them all mainly through Izzy. It was she who mentioned to Noah that I'd left the Army, and he called me up and invited me in for a chat. Said he was looking for someone to run the estate, and he thought I'd be an ideal candidate. I was floored—it wasn't really in my line of business, but I like to think he saw something in me I couldn't see in myself."

He smiles, but there's a touch of vulnerability there. I'm sure he's right, and Noah saw in him a wounded soldier who needed rescuing. Rescuing is what Noah does best.

"Do you enjoy your job now?" I ask him.

"Yes, there's always something to do, we're helping animals, and it's busy there without being crazy. Plus, of course, I get to see you." His eyes twinkle.

"Stop it," I scold. "You're not supposed to be flirting with me."

"Why not?"

"Because this is strictly a business arrangement," I remind him.

"I understand, but I'm not an automaton. Girls aren't the only ones who need warming up."

"Warming up?" His expression amuses me.

"Don't smirk," he says. "I've never had a one-night stand. I like to get to know a girl first."

His words remind me that we're sleeping together tonight. I keep forgetting then remembering and receiving this little shiver all the way down my back.

"So, anyway," he says, "enough about me. I want to know more about you."

I chew my sandwich. "I'm not used to talking about myself."

"Daniel wasn't interested?"

I shrug. I don't want to think about Daniel.

"Well, I am," Marc tells me. "So you haven't been to Hawke's Bay before. Have you traveled much?"

Chapter Eight

Fitz

Poppy eats her sandwich, obviously thinking about how to reply to my question. She usually wears jeans and T-shirts for work because she's with the animals, but today she's wearing a pale gray pantsuit with a cream blouse. She's braided her glorious hair into one long plait that hangs over her right shoulder. She looks amazing. I'd be happy to get started on the baby-making and do her on the table, but I think flight attendant Chris might have something to say about that.

She's still thinking silently. I understand her reticence. It took a lot of courage for me to admit to what happened with Mel. Not even Noah or Leon knows about her, although it wouldn't surprise me if Izzy's told Hal.

I suppose it's because I'm ashamed of what happened. All relationships take work, and I was so caught up with my own feelings about the accident that Mel must have felt as if she'd taken a back seat. Maybe Poppy's right, and if Mel had truly loved me, she'd have stayed by my side to help me through it, but I certainly don't consider myself blameless. I was selfish, and I don't want my friends to know that.

So why did I tell Poppy? Especially since I'm planning to take her to bed?

It was instinctive; I want to deepen our relationship. What I said was true—guys need warming up, too, and although I find her physically attractive and I've fantasized about making love to her ever since I've met her, I don't want this to be all about sex. And the only way to make it more is to talk.

I'm not a natural at it, but at least I'm trying.

I wonder whether she's asking herself the same questions about admitting things to me. She's certainly pondering what to say. Maybe she feels that because I've opened up, she should, too. I hope so.

"I did my OE when I was twenty," she replies eventually, referring to the 'overseas experience' that many young Kiwis go on either before or after university. "I was… having a bit of trouble."

I choose another sandwich. "What kind of trouble?"

"Well, you know that Albie and I… we're both… on the spectrum," she says. She rubs her nose. She doesn't like the phrase, and I don't either. It sets her apart from everyone else, as if she's different, and she's not. But I nod, because I don't want to interrupt her. "Dad is, too," she says, "and so I suppose he could spot it in the two of us. We're at the high-functioning end, but all three of us struggle with communication sometimes."

I've met Charlie King, and I would never have realized he had this problem, but I guess he's grown adept at covering it over the years. I've seen Albie crash headfirst into trouble because he's not been able to read other people, which means he's put his foot in it, so I'm guessing his father is the same.

"School was difficult for me," she continues, somewhat reluctantly. "It was difficult for Albie too, but he's a guy, and he was able to cover his awkwardness with his sense of humor and typical guy antics. I wasn't able to do that. I didn't make friends easily, and I didn't have a boyfriend all through school—I was far too shy. I was top of most of my classes, but my intelligence isolated me. I wasn't a sporty person, so I didn't fit in with that type either. I hated school, and I had no idea what to do with myself in the big wide world. I didn't want to go to university and waste time and money because I had no focus. I was sort of… lost."

"So you went traveling?"

She nods and sips her drink. "It was Dad's idea. Both he and Mom were convinced I'd find my calling in time, and that it was best not to rush into anything. Dad suggested I travel for a while. Mom wasn't that happy at first; she thought it would be dangerous for a twenty-year-old girl who wasn't very worldly-wise to travel on her own. But I was excited by the idea, and eventually she agreed."

"Where did you go?"

"I flew to London, traveled around England a bit, then went on to Europe, through France, Germany, Italy. I enjoyed it, looking around art galleries and museums, learning some of the languages, but I was conscious it wasn't solving anything. And then I went to India, and I ended up in Nepal."

That surprises me. "You liked it there?"

"I loved it. I went to Kathmandu, and to Boudhanath and Swayambhunath, which are the two most important religious places for Tibetans living outside Tibet. And I was walking through the busy streets of Swayambhunath when I heard sounds of drums and tubes. I rounded the corner and found that they were coming from a beautiful monastery, painted in bright colors, where monks were having a puja, or a prayer. I spoke to a Tibetan guard at the gate, and he said I could enter the temple and join the puja. I sat there for over two hours, watching two hundred monks praying and playing on these instruments. I ended up staying there for two weeks."

Her eyes are alight and filled with dreamy memories. I'm spellbound by her expression and her words. It obviously had a profound impact on her.

"So these were Tibetan monks?" I ask.

"Yes, they'd come from Tibet after the Chinese invasion in 1959. It took them a month to cross the Himalayas. Parents from Tibet often sent their children to Nepal to keep them safe, and to get them education and food. There are Tibetan monasteries all over Nepal that are supported by Buddhists from countries like America, Australia, and countries in Europe."

"So what did you do during your stay?"

"By sheer luck, I'd arrived two days before a ten-day-long celebration. They celebrated 'bardo', which is a Tibetan word for 'in between', which is the state in which souls stay when the body dies and before they are reborn. The lamas—the older Tibetan monks—had special meditations, and I was invited to watch. There were dances and singing, and they wore costumes and masks."

"It sounds amazing."

"It was. I loved it. But the best part of it was that over fifty of the monks were small children."

"Really?"

"Yes, and maybe because most of them couldn't speak English, I didn't have trouble communicating like I usually do. They kept asking me to sing and dance with them, and I sat with them and taught them some English words."

"That's how you got into teaching," I say softly, and she nods.

"I've found with children that I don't experience the problems I do with adults. There doesn't tend to be any nuance with kids—they usually say what they mean, and they don't expect you to read between the lines."

"So when you got back from Nepal, you took a teaching degree?"

"Yes. It was hard work, but I enjoyed it, and I was very focused. I worked in Auckland for a couple of years, then eventually moved up the bay. Mom and Dad still live in Auckland, but they spend most weekends up here with Brock and Matt and the others, and it's just so beautiful here."

"Do you think you'll ever go back to Nepal?" I ask.

"Maybe. It had extra meaning, though, because of what I was going through at the time. It would still be lovely, but it wouldn't be the same, you know?"

I nod. "Do you miss teaching?"

She leans back in her chair and sighs. "Sometimes, although I still have a lot of contact with children, without any of the responsibility. Teaching is hard work and exhausting. The adage of them having all that time off with school holidays is rubbish—most of that time I spent reorganizing the classroom, planning lessons, or going on professional development. There's so much paperwork involved now, too, so many reports. I don't miss that."

It makes more sense to me now, why she so wants a child. She feels she connects more to children, and they don't judge her the way adults do. I guess she's hoping she'll get unconditional love from her child the way she obviously hasn't from a man.

"So tell me about Daniel," I say.

Her expression immediately becomes even more guarded than usual. "What do you want to know?"

"Where did you meet him?"

"At school. He's the deputy principal at the primary school I worked at."

"Oh?" I know it takes time to work your way up in education, so this surprises me. "How old is he?"

"Forty."

Ten years older than she is. Again, I'm surprised.

And suddenly, I know what happened, and it all falls into place.

"He was married," I say, and I can tell from her expression I'm right. "You had an affair?"

"No. I refused to sleep with him, so eventually he left his wife." Her gaze is cautious; she's waiting for me to pass judgment on her.

"He must have loved you very much," I murmur.

She blinks a couple of times, and her eyes glisten. She drops her gaze to her glass. "He never loved me. I think he saw something in me that wasn't there. He thought I was mysterious and elusive, and that once he got to know me, he'd uncover something rare and significant. He didn't realize there was nothing special beneath the surface."

Anger unfurls in me like a snake. "That's bullshit. Of course you're special. He's like a miner looking for diamonds while wearing a blindfold. Just because he didn't discover something he considered precious doesn't mean it isn't there."

She lifts her gaze to mine then, and I can see her thoughts as sure as if they're glittering fish swimming behind her eyes. She's worried I'm the same—that I'm drawn to her quietness and her mystique, thinking it masks a fascinating soul, and that when I get to know her, I'll discover she's hollow inside.

I have a bite of my sandwich. "Fuck him. He's an idiot."

She gives a short laugh. "We concur on that, anyway."

"Did he go back to his wife?"

She nods.

"What a cunt."

"Marc!"

"Well. He is. And she took him back! Jeez."

She rolls her eyes. "I'm glad she did. At least I didn't ruin his marriage."

"You didn't do anything. How can you blame yourself?"

"I was the other woman, Marc. I have to take responsibility for what happened."

Understanding dawns. "The staff at the school blame you?"

She picks at the lettuce in her sandwich. "They assume I seduced him and asked him to leave his wife. I didn't. He came after me, and I suppose I was flattered he wanted me enough to give up his family."

"You loved him?"

"I thought I did. Until he was cruel to me."

I breathe slowly to keep down the rage I feel against Daniel Maggothead. All that matters is Poppy, and making her feel better about herself.

I push aside our plates and drinks and lean my forearms on the table. "Come here."

She stares at me blankly. "What?"

I reach out, take the end of her braid in my left hand, and wind it around my fingers. She watches me warily. When I get to the point where it tightens, she says, "Ow."

"So move forward," I direct, winding it again.

She leans on the table, and her lips slowly curve up as she realizes what I'm doing. I wind the braid until she's close to me, until our lips are only six inches apart.

"What are you doing?" she whispers.

Her eyes are a beautiful green. Her pale skin has a few freckles across her nose. I drop my gaze to her mouth, which is pale pink and looks extremely kissable. "We've got to start somewhere."

"But—"

I close the gap and press my lips to hers.

She inhales, but she doesn't pull away. Conscious that Chris could appear through the curtain at any moment, I keep it PG-13, but take my time, giving her butterfly kisses, soft and gentle. After so long watching her, wanting her, it's amazing to finally be so close to her, so intimate. God, her lips are soft, like the clouds outside the window, and I have to stifle a groan that threatens to rise within me.

It's been a tough year, and after Poppy turned me down back in June, I doubted I'd ever get the chance to do this. But here I am, kissing her. It feels like a gift, as if an angel has granted me a wish. The sun slants through the windows of the plane, coating us in warm bars of gold. I can smell Poppy's perfume, something light and flowery. I close my eyes, imagining how it's going to feel later, when I'll be able to undo the buttons on her blouse and slide it off her shoulders, kiss her breasts, and make love to her. This is a little like what heaven feels like, I think, as the plane passes through the clouds, heading for the jewel of Hawke's Bay. I never thought I'd associate this place with happiness again, but Poppy has blown away all the dark feelings, and suddenly all I can think of is being there with her, and having her all to myself.

Chapter Nine

Poppy

After the plane lands, we pick up the hire car, and Marc drives us to the new Ark.

It's extremely difficult for me to concentrate after the kiss. I hadn't expected that at all, and I half-regret giving in to him. He took me by surprise, and I wasn't prepared. I have to keep my wits about me this week. I don't believe that men are the only ones who can have sex without getting their emotions involved, but equally it's going to take willpower of iron to maintain the kind of control I'm going to need to keep myself distant from him. The way Marc wound my braid around his hand and pulled me toward him... the touch of his lips... it made my heart race. What on earth is it going to feel like when we take off our clothes; when he's touching me, kissing my skin; when he's inside me?

I shiver as he takes the turnoff for the new Ark and resolve to put the memory of the kiss out of my mind or I'm going to get nervous.

As if I'm not already.

The Ark is in a beautiful location on the outskirts of Hastings, although I don't think its views are quite as breathtaking as ours in the Bay of Islands.

As it's Sunday, the site is clear of building crew, but Ashton, the estate manager, has called in to meet us, and he gives us a brief tour. It's coming along well; they've completed the main office block, and the veterinary center is nearly finished. He's very interested in the petting farm, and asks to meet with me later in the week to discover what's worked and what hasn't, in case they decide to have one further down the line.

We don't want to keep him on his day off, so after an hour we part ways, promising to return the next morning around nine.

Marc makes a quick phone call, then returns to the car and buckles himself in. "So… time to discover our magical destination for the week." He gives me an impish smile.

I've asked him a couple of times where we're staying, but he's refused to tell me. I'm guessing it's a flash hotel in Hastings somewhere. It's difficult to know how to handle the fact that I'm wealthy when I'm with a guy. Daniel used to make a show of taking me to expensive restaurants and hotels as if he felt the need to make the point that he could afford to do it, even though I knew he was having to pay child support and alimony.

I don't know what Marc's like with money. He has a Ford Ranger Raptor because he spends most of his time bumping over unmade roads and fields. It's a beautiful car but it's covered in mud most of the time. He has a couple of nice suits, but he doesn't have the fancy sports cars and watches that Leon has, and Izzy once told me he rents a small apartment on the edge of town, so he doesn't own his own home. I doubt he's rolling in money, and I wouldn't want him to think, like Daniel, that he has to try to impress me.

I like having money; I like owning a nice car, living in a comfortable, quiet home, buying nice clothes, but it's not the be-all and end-all for me. I know it's easy to say that when you have it, and like the other members of my family I make regular donations to charities because I often feel guilty that I'm wealthy, but I'm not the type of girl who has to be bought diamonds to be impressed. Daniel bought me diamond earrings for my birthday, and it clearly meant nothing. I'd rather have paste diamonds from a guy who loves me.

To my surprise, Marc doesn't head into Hastings, but instead turns east, through the tiny town of Haumoana, and continues along the coast. Wherever we're going, it's not in a city.

The road bends around to the right, but he slows, indicates left, even though there aren't any other cars, and turns off the main road and onto a narrow lane heading toward the sea. There's only one building at the end of the lane. It's a lighthouse.

I turn to stare at Marc. "We're staying there?"

He laughs. "It's a lot more isolated than I expected." He gives me a rueful look. "If it's too bleak, I'm happy to see if I can find us somewhere in Hastings."

"Marc, it's amazing. Oh my God." We're surrounded on both sides by the sea, which breaks on the limestone rocks to spray the road.

At the end, in front of the lighthouse, is a car. As we pull up, a woman in her fifties with gray hair in a bob comes through the front door of the lighthouse and smiles.

We get out, and she comes over and says, "Marc?"

"Yes, you must be Fiona." He shakes her hand. "This is Poppy."

"Hello." I shake her hand, my face flushing as I realize she must be assuming we're a couple. Well, I suppose we are, for this week. Maybe if I think like that, it'll make this easier.

"Please, come in," she says, leading the way into the lighthouse. Marc gestures for me to precede him, and I follow Fiona inside. Oh, it's beautiful. The ground floor is a living area, with a sofa and a small TV, and a tiny kitchen with a sink, a microwave, a fridge, and a bench to prepare food. Stairs curve up to the first floor, which has a bedroom with a double bed and a tiny bathroom. Above that is a viewing room, with a sofa facing folding doors that open out onto a balcony overlooking the sea. In front of us there's only the vast expanse of the Pacific Ocean. If we sailed out from this point, the next place we'd hit would probably be Chile.

There's so much sky that I'm a little dizzy, but I also feel liberated at the sense of space.

I turn to Marc, who has a look of such hope on his face that my heart wants to break. "It's amazing," I whisper. "Absolutely perfect."

"I'm so glad," Fiona says brightly, giving Marc the key. "There's a lovely bar that serves great seafood back in Haumoana, and a bakery that does takeaway rolls and sandwiches. And there's plenty of food for breakfast in the cupboards, bread in the bread bin, and butter, milk, bacon, and eggs in the fridge, so please help yourselves."

"Thank you so much." Marc leads the way back downstairs and sees Fiona out, and I hear her get in her car and head back up the lane. He comes back in and stands in the center of the room, his hands stuffed in the pockets of his jeans. "I'm glad you like it."

"I love it," I say softly. "It was a brilliant idea."

He glances around. "I wanted something a bit special for the conception of our son or daughter." His gaze comes back to me, mischievous and amused.

I think of our kiss earlier, and my heart bangs against my ribs. His expression softens. "Don't panic."

"I'm not," I lie.

He moves a bit closer, looking down at me. He's quite a bit taller, maybe six-two, with broad shoulders and a vast expanse of chest. My fingers tingle at the thought of tugging up his shirt and sliding onto his warm skin. He fills my thoughts and my senses, and I'm getting to the stage where I can't think of anything else when he's close to me.

"We don't have to do anything you don't want to," he states gently. "I'm sorry about the kiss this morning. I have a feeling that threw you."

"It did. A bit."

"I'm sorry."

I shake my head. I don't know how to explain that I liked it, but I'm worried more like that will mean I'm not going to find it easy to keep my heart in its padlocked box.

Sex for me has usually been hard and fast, with the guy desiring the quickest route possible to his destination. I've always thought foreplay a creation of moviemakers and romance novelists, like heroes who are kind and considerate rather than only concerned with themselves. Daniel declared he loved me, but his lovemaking was as uninspired and brief as my few previous lovers. He seemed to want to sleep with me purely to achieve a climax. Men seem to assume women find it sexy to be pounded into, and either don't know or don't care that it takes some gentler focus on certain areas of a woman's body to enable her to orgasm.

Marc's comment a few days ago when he asked, "If you communicate what you like and what turns you on, why should it be any different with the man in your life?" was an eye-opener for me. None of the men I've been with have seemed interested in discussing my pleasure, and as a result, I've never thought to bring up the subject. I feel sort of stupid now, as if, as a modern woman, I should have put my pleasure on an equal level with a man's, but the truth is I just didn't think about it. I assumed this is how it is. Men don't pick up their socks, they sit with their legs wide apart, they eat a packet of chips in two mouthfuls, and they climax before a woman. It's nature, and a woman would be foolish to expect anything else.

Despite Marc's promises of multiple orgasms, I realize now I'd still expected him to be the same as the other men in my life. But even that one kiss was different from any other kiss I've ever had. If I'm honest with myself, I've never been super keen on kissing. Guys have always wanted to force their tongue into my mouth, and wet, squelchy kisses turn my stomach. But he was so gentle, his lips warm and dry as he pressed them to mine. I've never been kissed like it.

I want him to kiss me like that again. Is that terrible?

He's watching me with a strange smile, and I don't know what to say, so instead I move closer, slide my arms around his waist, and give him a hug, resting my cheek on his chest.

"Aw," he says, and wraps his arms around me.

He smells of aftershave and freshly washed clothes and the scent of warm, clean male. My mouth is an inch from the V of his open-necked shirt, and I'm tempted to turn my head and press my lips to his skin. But even though we're here for sex, and I don't think he'd mind, I'm too shy to do it.

He lifts a hand, though, tucks a finger under my chin, and lifts it until I meet his eyes. He studies mine for a moment, then lowers his lips to mine.

I close my eyes, breathing in his scent, and concentrate on the kiss. He's so gentle. He holds his lips there, then presses them again, long, tender kisses that give me a deep ache inside—I'm not sure if it's in my heart or further down. Maybe both.

He kisses me for a long time, while the sun pours over us like melted butter, and seagulls swoop and cry overhead. He doesn't seem in any rush, and I think I could stand here forever like this, being kissed, my arms around his waist, enjoying being so close to him. It's so innocent, just a brushing of our lips, but I feel as if someone's poured hot water into my veins. Heat rises in me, and by the time he lifts his head, I'm yearning for more.

But he studies my face, smiles, and says, "Why don't we go to that bar Fiona mentioned and get some dinner?"

I nod, half disappointed, half relieved. I know he's taking it slow on purpose for me. I'm so incredibly touched. But it's only putting off the inevitable. Later, he's going to take me into the bedroom above us, undress me, and make love to me. He's going to brush his tanned hands across my skin, and maybe his lips, too. I already know he's going to be gentle and slow, and I'm starting to think he might have been right when he said he gives a woman pleasure every time he has sex.

Oh dear.

Chapter Ten

Fitz

Poppy's nervous.

I suppose that was to be expected. I'm surprised, though. She's thirty, and she told me she's had a few partners, so even if she hasn't had a one-night stand, I would've thought the notion of a fling wouldn't have bothered her.

Most—if not all—of the women I've slept with have been sexually liberated, in the sense that they believe their pleasure is as important as the guy's, and they expect the man they're sleeping with to agree. They know how to touch themselves and are happy to pass that knowledge on to their partner, so for me sex has always been a two-way street. It's not about me being an expert, but I've watched and learned, and I've never had any complaints.

If Poppy's declaration about climaxing during sex wasn't enough of a clue, her nervousness is beginning to suggest to me that her sex life has been far from satisfying. What's sad is her conviction that her experience has been normal. How many women out there are in the same position? How many are with men who roll over after sex and fall asleep, leaving them aching for fulfilment?

I want to talk to her about it, but at the moment I'm worried that if I bring up the subject of us sleeping together, she'll get to the stage where her anxiousness will develop into full-blown panic and she'll make me sleep on the sofa, so instead I decide not to mention it, and instead to concentrate on helping her to relax.

It turns out Fiona was right, and the bar down the road produces some damn fine fish and seafood dishes. Poppy chooses a paella, and I go for citrus pan-fried snapper with lemon mash, although we share the dishes and end up eating half of each. It's a beautiful spring evening; the sun is setting, and out to sea the ocean is turning dramatic shades of orange, red, and purple. Closer to shore, the waves break beneath us, and from our table by the window we can see the white spray painting the rocks.

The bar is basic and homely, with bare floorboards and wooden tables covered with checkered cloths, but there's something romantic about the atmosphere. The waiter lights a candle and places it between us, love songs are playing softly in the background, and there are several other couples having dinner around us, holding hands and looking lovingly into each other's eyes.

We don't hold hands, but there's something happening between us. Even though we don't talk about what's going to happen when we get back to the lighthouse, I know it's on her mind, and it's certainly on mine. She's slipped off her jacket and hung it over the back of her chair, and the blouse she's wearing is unbuttoned low enough that I catch a glimpse of cleavage. The skin there is pale and unblemished, and I know it's going to be warm, and touched with the scent of her light, flowery perfume.

Her neck is smooth, and I keep thinking about kissing up to her ear and nuzzling there. Would she like that? I want to find out. I want to discover what makes her tick. What makes her sigh. I want to see what she smells like, what she tastes like, what sounds she makes when she comes. Will she be silent during sex, or will she sigh my name? I like the way she uses my name when everyone else calls me Fitz; it's as if she's discovered a secret, as if our relationship is private, special. Even Mel always called me Fitz.

I want to take the elastic from the end of her braid and unravel it, spread it across her shoulders, bury my face in it. I want to kiss her, and see whether I can persuade her to use her tongue. I want to slide inside her. God, I want to be inside her.

She has a sip of her wine and lifts her green eyes to mine. "Stop it," she scolds.

I lift my eyebrows. "What?"

"Looking at me as if you're thinking about me with no clothes on."

It's the first time either of us has mentioned sex. I've kept the conversation on movies and music and traveling, determined to get her to relax.

"I'm not gonna lie," I tell her. "It has entered my head once or twice."

She gives me a wry look and pushes her plate to the side. "Once or twice?"

"All right, I've barely thought about anything else. Can I help it when you're so gorgeous?"

She gives a bashful smile. "You don't have to seduce me, Marc. I'm a sure thing, remember?"

The thought sends a ripple of desire through me, but I ignore it and point to her plate with my fork. "You're not finishing that?"

"It's lovely, but…" She gives a little laugh and blows out a breath. "I'm too nervous."

"Really?" I tip my head to the side. "You shouldn't be. It's only me."

"Mm. I know. That's kind of the problem."

"What do you mean?" I'd assumed she would have been nervous with any partner.

She turns the stem of her wine glass with her fingers, giving me a puzzled look. "Because I like you. And even though this is just temporary, I want you to… like me too."

"I do like you."

"No, I mean… you know… in bed."

I remember what she said about being worried she'd disappoint me. "Honestly," I tell her, "I can't think of a single way you could possibly disappoint me in bed."

She rubs her nose. "I have wondered… maybe there's something, you know, wrong with me. Because I'm on the spectrum, maybe it's more difficult for me to… you know."

"Have an orgasm?"

"Mm." She chews her bottom lip.

I study her for a moment. It looks as if talking about orgasms over dinner is going to be a thing with Poppy and me. Fair enough. If we're going to talk about it, I'm going to take my time and do it right.

"Do you want a dessert?" I ask her.

She looks surprised. "Er…"

"How about we share something?"

"Okay."

I call the waitress over, and order a chocolate pudding and two more glasses of wine. Normally I wouldn't have a second glass if I was driving, but bearing in mind we didn't pass a single car on the way here,

I figure another unit for the five-minute drive on a deserted road is going to be relatively safe.

When the waitress departs, I lean on the table and study the woman who is beginning to fascinate me more than any other woman I've ever met and tell her, "I'm ninety-nine-point-nine percent convinced there's nothing wrong with you."

"That still leaves point one of a percent."

"All right, then, I'm a hundred percent convinced."

"I don't know how you can be, if ten to fifteen percent of all women have never had an orgasm."

"I know. I've read the stats. And I wish there was enough time for me to prove to them they're wrong, but unfortunately there's only one of me, and anyway, I'm only interested in one woman."

Her lips curve up. "I can't make my mind up whether you're confident or arrogant."

"Jesus, I'm not arrogant. It's nothing to do with the guy. Well, it's partly to do with the guy, obviously, but…" I frown. "What I'm trying to say is that from what I've read, there are hardly any women who are physically unable to achieve an orgasm. There are various reasons some find it more difficult. Often it's psychological; they're brought up to believe touching themselves and giving themselves pleasure is wrong, so they don't masturbate. How can you tell a partner what you like if you don't know yourself?" She looks out the window. "Is that what happened with you?" I ask gently.

She shakes her head. "My parents were always relatively open about sex. They never implied there was anything dirty or wrong about it."

I follow her gaze, to where two seagulls are pushing and shoving each other for prime position on the highest rock. It gives me a thought. "What about Summer?"

Her gaze comes back to me then, somewhat sharp. "What do you mean?"

"She's what… seven, eight years older than you? So you were going through puberty when she was at university and going with Zach. Did that have any effect on you?"

The waitress comes back with our wine, but Poppy doesn't even notice, lost in thought, looking out to sea again. I sip the Pinot Noir, sensing I'm closing in on the problem.

"It was almost the opposite," she says softly. "I love Summer. She's always been great with Albie and me. And because she knew we both struggled socially, she's always made an extra effort to help. She'd talk to me about boys and try to give me tips on how to talk to them, without realizing I had no comprehension of what she was saying. She was open about sex, too, because I think she wanted to take away the fear for me, but all it did was baffle me. At the time, when I was in my teens, I didn't understand why anyone would want to let a guy do that to them. I didn't have a boyfriend until I was nineteen. In the end, I had sex because I just wanted to get it over with and done with, and it was as awful and painful and messy and embarrassing as I'd feared. And it's never really been any different. I slept with Daniel because he was unrelenting, and I suppose I was beginning to be puzzled by the passion you see in the movies, and I thought I'd been unlucky and was missing out on something, but it was no different with him. So I've never liked sex very much."

Her gaze comes back to me. "The things you've told me," she continues, "I desperately want to believe they can be true, but I suppose I'm worried that's just how it's going to be for me." She gives a little, helpless shrug.

I'm speechless for the second time in as many days, and say nothing while the waitress returns with our chocolate pudding and places it between us with two spoons. When she goes, I hand Poppy one of the spoons and pick up the other, and we both delve into the chocolate sponge. It breaks open, revealing a lava flow of molten chocolate.

Poppy eats a mouthful with a sigh. "I'm sorry," she says. "I shouldn't say things like that. I'll end up giving you performance anxiety."

I laugh, scoop up some of the sauce with the pudding, and eat it. It's delicious. "That's one thing I'm not worried about."

"I'd feel terrible if I didn't… you know… and you felt bad about it."

"Christ. Poppy, that's not going to happen."

"You don't know that…"

"I do." I hold her gaze.

She blinks, her brows drawing together. "I don't understand how you can be so confident."

"Because you're going to show me how you like to be touched. And I'm going to take my time. I don't care if it takes all evening, or even all week, to get it right." I reach out and take her hand for the first time. "You've got nothing to worry about. Leave everything to me.

After saying that, there are several things you can do to help. I know it's impossible to ask you not to be nervous. But have a glass of wine. Try to relax. Enjoy yourself. Stop worrying about me—tonight I want you to concentrate on yourself. I'll enjoy it no matter what happens." She laughs. "And most importantly," I conclude, "talk to me. It's the easiest way to make sure I get it right."

She lowers her gaze to the pudding and has another bite. A smear of chocolate sauce on her lip makes me ache to lean forward and lick it off.

"One more thing," I tell her, pointing my spoon at her. "No faking it."

She scratches her nose. "I shouldn't have told you I did that."

"You won't need to do it with me, if you talk to me."

She has another spoonful, and meets my eyes again. For the first time, I can see that her nerves are fading, to be replaced by excitement, and—something that gives me even more hope—a flicker of desire. She's thinking about going to bed with me, and she's excited about it. The wine's beginning to have an effect, and so, hopefully, are my words.

I scoop up another spoonful of sauce. "I'm tempted to smuggle some of this back to the lighthouse."

"I know what you mean. It'd be nice to have a supply for a midnight snack."

"Actually I was thinking about how fun it would be to drizzle it over you and then lick it off."

She stops with the spoon halfway to her mouth and stares at me.

"Oh come on," I scoff, "one of your boyfriends must have done the whipped cream thing. Sprayed it on with a can and then licked it off."

Her expression tells me that's never happened. In fact, the shocked look on her face tells me it's never even entered her head.

"Fuck me," I mumble. "I'm definitely going to do that at some point." I push the dish with the last spoonful of pudding across to her.

She finishes off the mouthful, her eyes dancing, licks her lips, and gives a little laugh. It's such a beautiful sound that I resolve to make her laugh like that every day from now on.

And suddenly, I can't wait any longer. I want to crush my lips to hers, I want her body under mine. I want to make her come so hard it feels like a firework exploding, wiping away any thought of the poor excuse for men who've passed through her life like wet firecrackers.

"Finish your wine," I tell her softly. "It's time to go."

Chapter Eleven

Poppy

Marc refuses to let me pay for dinner, then leads me across the road to the shop. Fiona has left us a variety of food and drinks, but I prefer trim milk in my tea, and Marc declares he wants some chocolate, so we wander around the shop putting odds and ends into the basket—a bag of chips, a couple of bars of dark chocolate, a few bottles of wine.

He then stops at the refrigerator, opens the door, and extracts a can of aerosol cream. He meets my gaze as he puts it in the basket, smirks, and takes the basket from me before heading for the till.

Holy moly. My head is spinning. I thought he was joking.

"Don't look so alarmed," he says as we walk back to the car.

"I'm not alarmed." I'm terrified. This is so far out of my comfort zone, it's almost in the northern hemisphere. Where is he going to want to spray the whipped cream?

We get back in the car, and I buckle myself in. My heart is pounding, and I've broken out in a sweat, even though it's grown cool since we came out.

Marc sighs as he heads the car onto the road toward the lane to the lighthouse. Then he reaches out and takes my hand. "Are you okay? Are you hyperventilating?"

"I'm sorry. It was the spray cream. It tipped me over the edge."

He gives a short laugh and lifts my hand, bringing my fingers to his lips. He kisses them lightly before lowering them back down. "I'm the one who should apologize. I promised myself I'd take it slow. Look, remember, we don't have to do anything you don't want to do. And we go at your pace. Okay? This is all about you. If you change your mind at any point, you only have to say. You're not going to upset me, and I won't be angry. We're doing this because you want a baby, and ultimately that's got to be the primary goal."

I look out of the window, into the dark night. Truth is, I'd almost forgotten I was doing this to try to get pregnant.

I glance across at him. He's concentrating on the road, a slight frown on his brow. He's incredibly handsome, in an insouciant, devil-may-care kind of way. I think part of me is shocked a guy like this would be interested in me. Daniel was forty, with a receding hairline, and although he was relatively good looking, he spent a lot of time at the gym, carefully maintaining his physique.

I don't think Marc goes to the gym, but his job means that half his day is spent outdoors doing physical work. His shirt clings to his biceps and his forearms where he's rolled up the sleeves, and his arms are tanned and honed. I know he has a tight butt because I've stared at it often enough. He was in the Army, and he said he was into sports. At school, guys like this wouldn't have looked at me twice. I was small and skinny with Pippi Longstocking hair, and so bad socially I could barely hold a conversation. The thought that one of the rugby guys would not only glance my way, but agree to get me pregnant…

And that's the first time it really sinks in. I didn't really comprehend it before.

Marc's going to have sex with me, and he's going to try to get me pregnant.

Laughter rises inside me, like bubbles in a glass of champagne, and bursts forth from me before I get a chance to stop it. He glances across at me, amused. "What's so funny?"

"Nothing." The laughter won't stop, though, and by the time he pulls up at the lighthouse, I'm giggling like a schoolgirl.

He stops the car, turns off the engine, and unbuckles his seatbelt. My laughter ends as abruptly as it began, and I pick up the few items we bought and hug them to me like a shield.

He doesn't try to touch me, though. "Come on," he says gently. "It's cold out here. Let's get inside."

We let ourselves in the lighthouse, which is pleasantly warm, as we left the heat pump on when we went out. Marc turns on the lamp while I hang my jacket by the door. My hands are shaking. This is so ridiculous. I'm going to have to do something or he's not going to be able to get near me for the tremors.

"Hold on a minute," I tell him as he turns toward me. "I have a present for you."

I run up the stairs to the bedroom, open my case, and retrieve it, then come back down the stairs. He's taken off his jacket and is standing by the window, looking out at the moonlight on the ocean.

"Look at that," he whispers. "A pathway to the stars. How amazing is that?"

"It's beautiful." I stand beside him and hold out the present. It's a sparkly silver paper bag containing a rectangular cardboard box, and as I pass it to him the liquid sloshes from one end to the other.

His eyebrows rise, and he takes the box out of the bag. It's a bottle of Laphroaig whisky, his favorite.

"Jesus," he says. "It's a thirty-year-old."

"Yeah. It's supposed to be really nice."

"That's the understatement of the year." His gaze slides to me. He knows his whisky—he must realize it cost nearly fifteen hundred dollars. For a second I wonder whether he's going to turn it down, but instead his face breaks into an amazing smile. "Thank you."

"Least I could do for what you've offered to do for me," I say shyly. "Shall we have a glass?"

"You don't mind? These are very peaty."

"Oh, Dad's a big fan of Islay malts. I've been well schooled."

He grins. "Next time I see Charlie, I'm going to shake his hand."

"He'd like that." It's the truth, I think, as I watch Marc retrieve two tumblers from the cupboard above the sink and begin to undo the bottle. Dad's met Marc several times when he's come to the Ark. Last time was at Hal and Izzy's wedding, when he told me, "That Fitz is a solid guy, Poppy," after Marc gave him a tour of the new buildings with Jack at his heels, then offered to play football in the field with Summer's two boys. If I'm honest with myself, Dad giving him the okay was the moment the idea sprang into my head about asking Marc to be a sperm donor. I knew right then that if Dad thought he was a good guy, I couldn't go far wrong in having him as the father of my child.

And then the second realization of the night hits me. If things go according to plan, I could be leaving the lighthouse at the end of the week already pregnant.

"Penny for them," Marc says, handing me one of the tumblers.

Normally, I don't say what's on my mind, because I'm never sure what people's reactions will be. But he asked me to talk to him, to be open with him, and so I decide to tell the truth. "I was thinking that by the time we fly home, I could be pregnant."

He smiles. "That's the plan." He gestures at my glass. "Is it okay to have alcohol while you're trying?"

"Obviously, I wouldn't drink while I was pregnant, but there's no evidence it's harmful beforehand. I won't get plastered, but I could do with a little Dutch courage."

"Fair enough."

I lift the whisky glass to my nose and take a sniff. Mmm, sweet fruits—mandarin and mango, and a touch of coconut. I take a sip and taste orange and vanilla—it's amazing.

Marc runs his tongue across his teeth. "Fantastic."

"Mmm." I have another large mouthful. I've had two glasses of wine and I don't want to be comatose, but equally I'm desperate to relax.

He takes my hand. "Come with me."

My heart racing, I follow him as he climbs the steps. Is he going to want me to take my clothes off straight away? Will he let me put the light out? Oh God, I'm so nervous I think I'm going to be sick.

But he doesn't stop at the bedroom. Instead, he continues climbing to the first floor, and we emerge into the viewing room.

"Oh, wow." My jaw drops at the sight of the Pacific spread out before us. The light above us sweeps across the black blanket of the ocean, warning unwary sailors of the rocks below us. A thousand stars glitter in the night sky, while the moon, almost full, hangs there like a silver bauble.

Marc sits at the right-hand end of the sofa and, still holding my hand, pulls me down beside him. I curl up next to him, and he puts his arm around me, sliding down a little so his head rests on the back of the sofa, stretching out his legs. I can cope with this. He's warm and he smells nice, and it's good to be touching him at last.

We sip our whiskies and look out at the stars. "Have you ever been sailing?" he asks me. I shake my head. "Me neither," he replies. "Just never got into it. It must be amazing, being out on the ocean at night."

"Until there's a storm and you're trying to stay upright in six-foot waves."

He chuckles. "Yeah." He turns and kisses my forehead, then returns to sipping his whisky. "Tell me more about your visit to the monastery. Did it give you an interest in Buddhism?"

Surprised, I talk for a while about the services I attended, and the monks I spoke to who told me a little about their beliefs and philosophy. "I found it really interesting," I conclude. "I'm not about to take it up, but I did like some of the core philosophies. What about you, are you religious?"

He shakes his head. "When I was younger, Mom sometimes took Izzy and me to church at Easter and Christmas. I was fifteen when Dad died, and that changed everything for her. She spent a lot of her time cursing God for taking Dad away from her. Since then, I haven't set foot in a church."

"Do you have faith?"

He has a mouthful of whisky as he considers my question, then looks across at me. "I could start believing if I thought heaven might contain angels like you."

"I'm no angel," I whisper.

"The best girls aren't." He smiles.

My heart bangs against my ribs. His gaze drops to my mouth, but he makes no move to kiss me. I keep waiting for him to start his seduction, but for some reason he's holding back.

Then he lifts his gaze back to mine, and suddenly I understand. He *is* seducing me. He's been doing it all day. Talking to me, trying to relax me, encouraging me out of my shell, getting me to tell him about myself. And now he's waiting for me to give him a sign I'm ready. He's such a sweetheart. He's determined not to push me. He's leaving it up to me.

I finish off my whisky and put the glass on the floor. The firewater has spread through me, filing off the edges, and for the first time I feel excited rather than nervous. I'm going to do this. It's an amazing opportunity, and I'm not going to pass up the chance now I'm here.

Marc does the same, wiping his mouth with the back of his hand before placing his glass on the floor. He leans back, and I turn a little to face him. I lift a hand and cup his cheek, brushing my thumb against his five-o'clock shadow, enjoying the scrape of his bristles. Then I slide my fingers into his hair to pull his head down and bring his mouth to mine.

Chapter Twelve

Poppy

Our lips touch, and we both exhale with relief and satisfaction, our breaths mingling. His lips are warm and firm, and he places soft kisses across mine, showing me he's going to take his time. I can't stop a little shiver running through me, and I feel his lips curve up, but he doesn't stop.

He kisses me for a long time, breaking contact with my mouth at one point to kiss my cheeks, my eyebrows, my nose, and finally back to my lips. By this time, I'm in a dream, hazy with longing. He kisses me, and then, for the first time, I feel the touch of his tongue on my bottom lip.

I hesitate, not wanting to spoil the magic with a disgusting, sloppy kiss, but I don't want to disappoint him, so I part my lips to allow him access. But he doesn't force his tongue into my mouth like all the other men have before. He continues to press his lips to mine, following each time with a small brush of the tip of his tongue. He kisses across my bottom lip, then back across my top lip, as if he's exploring every fraction of an inch, and now I'm tingling all over, and more than ready to join in.

I follow his lead and do the same to him, kissing him, then touching my tongue to his lips, and he sighs. The thought that I'm turning him on pleases me, and when he eventually touches his tongue to mine, I respond with a shy thrust of my own. It's all the encouragement he needs to deepen the kiss, and he tightens his arms around me, sliding his tongue inside my mouth, but it's not disgusting or invasive; it's gentle and sensual and erotic. All the hairs on my body rise in response, and an ache begins deep inside me.

He's in no hurry, it seems, because he kisses me like that for ages, one arm tight around me, one hand in my hair, or stroking my face. I slide my arm around his waist and feel the hem of his shirt, pause as I debate whether to take this step, then think screw it, lift the fabric, and slip my hand onto his back.

Ooh, first contact. His skin is warm and smooth, and as I skate my fingers up a little, my thumb brushing up his side, I feel toned muscle. "Mmm," he murmurs against my mouth—he likes that, so I move my hand around his back and slide it up to between his shoulders, then draw my fingers down his spine. I like touching him, it feels possessive, as if I'm claiming him. At this moment, he doesn't belong to any other woman, and I can pretend he's mine.

He moves on the sofa, placing his hands beneath me, and then he lifts me, drawing me across his lap. I gasp as I find myself straddling him, but he doesn't give me time to think about it; he cups my head and brings my lips down to his, tightening his other arm around me until I'm flush against him. Oh my, I can feel his erection even through his jeans, hard against my mound.

Resting his hands on my hips, he strokes them up my back to my shoulders, down my arms, then back up, still kissing me leisurely. It feels as if we could do this all night, this gentle exploration of each other, and I adore it; I love that he's taking his time with me, that he's not rushing me. I sink my hands into his hair, and I do what he did to me earlier—kiss his cheek, his eyebrows, his forehead, down his nose. In response, he kisses my neck and up to my ear, nuzzles it, and touches his tongue to the lobe. A tiny moan I hadn't planned escapes my lips, and so he takes the lobe into his mouth and sucks gently, making me shudder.

Mmm, this is nice. I feel hazy and glowing, as if I'm floating in a warm sea that's carrying me away toward the horizon. It's fanciful, and I'm sure some of it is due to the whisky, but most of it is down to Marc's gentle hands and mouth, and the feelings he's arousing in me.

I love this slow adventure, but it's not intimate enough. I want to feel his skin again; I want to feel him against me. I bring my hands down to the top button of his shirt and move back to look at him. His lips curve up, so I push the button through the hole and move down to the next one, slowly unwrapping him. I'm concentrating too much on the shirt to meet his eyes, but I know he's watching me as I undo the last button and move the sides of his shirt apart.

I've seen him topless several times when he's been working around the Ark and he's gotten hot, but this is different; he's here, in front of me, and I can touch him. I place my palms on his chest and fan out my fingers, then brush them down his front, exploring his muscles with my fingertips, admiring the view as I go. His chest hair curls like the hair on his head, an attractive scatter across his ribs.

I lift my gaze to his. He looks a mixture of amused and aroused, his lips curved up, his eyes at half-mast. Keeping his eyes locked on mine, he lifts his hands to my blouse and begins to undo the buttons.

My breasts rise and fall faster than usual with my deep, fast breaths, but I sit still as he reaches the bottom of the blouse and parts the sides. He drops his gaze and sighs, then draws his fingers down my collarbone and over the top of my breasts where they're propped up in the pretty cream lacy bra.

He pushes the blouse off my shoulders, and I let it fall to the floor. Then he pulls me toward him again for another kiss.

This is slightly different; it's not hard or forceful, but there's heat behind it, and he cups the back of my head, keeping me there, as if he's determined to claim the kiss. I put my arms around his neck, leaning against him, and ohhh... the feel of my skin against his fires me up, and I sink my hands into his hair, clenching my fingers. His tongue slides against mine, and unbidden, my hips rock against his. Mmm... that's sexy, I feel hot and dizzy, filled with an odd ache, a deep desire I haven't felt before, not to this extent.

He cups my breasts and brushes his thumbs across the tips. When I arch my spine a little, he moves his hands around to my back, and then he unfastens my bra, the elastic loosening and setting me free. After drawing the straps down my arms, he tosses it aside, then cups my breasts with his warm hands.

Aaahhh... I exhale, my breath whispering across his lips. Gently, oh so gently, he strokes his thumbs across my nipples. I bite my lip, resting my forehead against his. This is so far removed from Daniel's hard and fast, sometimes almost cruel lovemaking, that I want to cry. He used to tug or suck on my nipples until it hurt, and it got to the stage where I didn't like him touching them, but this... This is something different. Marc circles around the edges of my nipples, then rolls the tips gently with the pad of his thumb, and they tighten to tight buds.

Pushing me upright, he kisses down my neck, then over my left breast as he cups it and covers the nipple with his mouth. His warm tongue washes over it, and I close my eyes and tip my head back, sinking my hand into his hair. Oh God, this is so heavenly… He takes his time kissing one nipple, then switches to the other, teasing with the tip of his tongue until my breathing deepens.

At that point, he moves back and kisses me again, running his hands over my body, and then, without any warning, he holds me tightly and gets to his feet, lowering mine carefully to the floor.

"Come on," he says, his voice low and husky. "I want you naked in my arms."

Breathless, I follow him down the steps to the bedroom, where he flicks on the bedside light, filling the tiny room with a warm glow. There's one window, facing toward the ocean, and briefly I see the light above us sweep across the sea's surface before Marc turns me and presses me up against the wall, and I forget everything except the man before me.

He kisses me while he lets his shirt slip off and then undoes his jeans, and I do the same with my trousers, letting them fall and kicking them off. Now we're only in our underwear, and when he presses up against me, he's all hot skin, height and breadth, hair and muscles, strength and power. I feel overwhelmed by him, my senses filled until I can't see, hear, or think of anything else.

His erection is hard against my belly, and I shiver as I think that soon he's going to be sliding inside me.

"Are you cold?" he murmurs, and I shake my head. He cups my face, looking into my eyes. "Are you all right? Do you want me to stop?"

"God, no." My reply is so vehement that he laughs, and he kisses me again, pushing his warm body against mine. He pulls the elastic back from the bottom of my braid and then unravels it and spreads my hair across my shoulders, giving a satisfied grunt. He likes my hair, and he sinks one hand into it as he continues to kiss me.

I slide my hands up his ribs and around to his back, brush them down either side of his spine, and onto his butt. The muscles there are tight and hard, and I give a low moan against his lips. I can't help it; it's automatic, but he groans in response and tears his lips from mine.

"You're driving me crazy," he says huskily, turning me from the wall and backing me toward the bed. "I want to go slow, but you're making it impossible."

"Sorry."

He laughs. "It wasn't a complaint." He pushes me gently back until I'm sitting on the bed, then turns me so I'm lying down, gesturing for me to move up onto the pillows. I wait for him to strip off his boxers and climb on top of me, but instead he moves to the end of the bed and gets on there, pausing as he leans over my legs.

"I have to taste you," he says in an apologetic tone. "I can't wait any longer. Is that all right?"

My head spins. "Yes," I say, my voice little more than a squeak.

"Good." He hooks his fingers into the side of my panties and strips them off deftly. Then he lowers himself down between my legs.

Oh dear God. Daniel never did this to me, not once. One of my old boyfriends had a go a few times, and I liked it, but he lost interest after several minutes. Somehow, I don't think Marc is going to lose interest. He kisses up my thigh, and his breath fans across me as he exhales. His hands press either side, parting me, and I cover my face with my hands as I feel his gaze on me, hot as his breath. And then he slides his tongue down into my folds. I can't stop the moan that leaves my lips. Ohhh... it feels amazing. My elbows fall to the side and I abandon myself to him, feeling his tongue teasing, his fingers joining in, sliding inside me.

I'm shocked that, only a few minutes later, pleasure begins to gather deep inside me. But why am I shocked? This is the most erotic thing I've ever experienced. I feel embarrassed and ashamed at how vehemently I protested to him that this never happens for women—he must have thought I was such a fool. I hate Daniel for making me think that. I resent him deeply.

But I'm not going to think about him now. Marc's tongue is working magic down there, and I can feel all the tiny muscles deep inside me winding tighter and tighter. Oh God, I think I'm going to come like this... I'm astounded, and I give a deep, shuddering breath. But as my climax approaches, he lifts up on the bed, moving up over me.

Giving deep, ragged breaths, I look up at him with some frustration, not sure whether to tell him how close I am. As soon as I look at him, though, I can tell that he knows. He slides off his boxers, and then leans either side of my shoulders, looking down at me with sympathy.

"Sorry," he murmurs. "Next time I'll take you all the way like that. But tonight, the first time you come, I want to be inside you."

Next time? He was serious—he gives a woman an orgasm every time he sleeps with her. For the first time, I understand why people make such a fuss about sex. If a woman were to have a real partner like this, I can see why she might never get out of bed.

Past the point of sensible speech, I let him kiss me, my face flaming at the thought of where his tongue has just been, and then he presses the tip of his erection into my folds.

"Ready?" he whispers. "You're sure?"

I nod, and he pushes his hips forward and slides inside me.

There's no pain at all; he's all the way up in one smooth thrust, filling me, and I close my eyes and groan as I feel myself stretch to accommodate him.

"Ah, Poppy." He kisses my lips, my cheek, my eyelids. "I've wanted to do this for so long." He withdraws a little and pushes forward again. My body seems on fire, as if it's been super-heated. Each thrust he gives sends a ripple of pleasure running through me, and I return his kiss hungrily, clutching my fingers in his hair.

He moves slowly, and it's so sensual, that slide of him through my sensitive skin, so much more erotic than having a guy hammer away. He should teach classes on this—he'd make a fortune.

Mmm… that feels so great… He pushes my knees higher, wrapping my legs around his waist, and stills for a moment as he pushes forward, oh God, so deep inside me… Then he begins moving again, kissing me, delving his tongue into my mouth. The sexy slide of it against mine matches the rhythm of his hips, and I'm sure I'm melting inside, turned into liquid pleasure by his slow, regular thrusts.

I run my hands up his arms, over his shoulders, down his back, loving the feel of his muscles moving, like a machine, with no sense of urgency. I never knew sex could feel like this… so loving… His mouth is tender, his lips and tongue teasing me… mmm…

His hips are moving a little faster now, but I don't mind, it feels good, it feels so good… Oh wow, pleasure is building again, tightening me up as if I have a spring inside. He lifts up onto his hands, and as he rocks his hips, he grinds against my clit… oh jeez… that feels amazing… Oh… I can feel it… way off in the distance…

"Oh God, don't stop, don't stop," I beg him. It's almost in reach… I've never felt like this before, never…

"I won't." He bends to kiss me. "I'm taking you all the way, honey. Relax and let it take you. Come for me."

I'm so close… I can't believe it… Oh God, don't stop… I let my knees fall to the side and my thighs open, and all there is in the world is Marc's hot mouth and that sweet spot in my belly that's so tight it's almost hurting… I want to… I can't quite… I'm almost…

He bends and covers my nipple with his mouth and sucks gently, and that tips me over the edge. Pleasure sweeps over me, everything tightens, and the pulses start, deep and powerful, forcing me to cry out loud as I clench around him. He kisses up to my mouth and covers it with his own, and I feel wholly his at that moment, I belong to him, as if he's climbed a mountain and planted a flag to claim me. He thrusts harder, but it doesn't hurt; somehow it just prolongs my orgasm, which seems to go on forever, making me cry out with its intensity.

He's plunging inside me, filling the air with the sound of our lovemaking, which is so hot I can't believe it, and then suddenly he stops and shudders, and his hips jerk… And with a burst of pure joy I realize he's coming inside me. Within a minute, goddamn it.

He groans, "Aaahhh…" His mouth is hot on mine, his body like rock beneath my fingers as all his muscles tense. He's feeling what I've just felt, and I've done that for him.

I don't know whether to be more amazed by my orgasm, or the fact that, at that moment, his life-giving fluid is spilling inside me. We could have made a baby tonight. Oh my God. I don't think I've ever been happier in my whole life.

Chapter Thirteen

Fitz

My body finally releases me, and I gasp and bury my face in Poppy's neck, breathing heavily. Oh, man. It felt amazing being inside her without the barrier of a condom, and made me so incredibly sensitive that it took all my willpower to make sure she came first before I gave in and let it happen.

But she did come—unless she faked it, and I'm pretty sure she didn't. I don't think she did, anyway. Can a man ever be one hundred percent sure?

I lift my head to look at her. To my shock, I see tears on her face.

"Hey." I push up onto my elbows and stare at her, startled. "What's the matter? Did I hurt you?" I was as gentle as I could have been, although I got carried away toward the end. But I thought she was enjoying it.

She shakes her head, her bottom lip trembling, as more tears gather on her lashes and then spill over like a rowboat going over a waterfall.

"Honey…" I try to kiss them away. "I'm sorry." Oh God. She did fake it, and now she feels guilty. Fuck. "It's okay. It was our first try. It takes time to get to know one another. I'll get better. Don't worry. You might still be pregnant." Saying it out loud gives me a funny feeling inside. I might have gotten her pregnant. Holy shit. That's a first.

"I know," she whispers. "That's partly why I'm crying."

I kiss her soft lips. "Only partly?"

"I feel so stupid."

I frown. "What?"

"You must think I'm such an idiot. Telling you women never have an orgasm during sex."

"You didn't fake it?"

She gives a short laugh. "No, Marc. I didn't fake it."

I kiss her, feeling a flood of relief. I was convinced I'd be able to prove her wrong, but it's nice to know for sure. "You promise?"

"I promise," she whispers.

I kiss her wet cheeks, then back to her mouth. "Don't cry."

"I can't help it."

"Aw." Carefully, I withdraw and stretch out beside her. "Here, pull your knees to your chest. It's supposed to keep the little swimmers inside for a bit longer."

Her big green eyes look up at me, and I feel a wash of tenderness and affection. I move up close and wrap my arms around her, pulling the duvet over us. "Come here."

Still curled up, she cuddles me, and I kiss the top of her head. She wipes her face, then rests her cheek on my shoulder.

"I could have knocked you up," I tell her.

That makes her laugh. "Oh Marc, you're so romantic."

"It's amazing though, when you think about it. That you can create life out of an act of pleasure." I trail my fingers up and down her spine, my eyelids drooping. Damn after-sex hormones.

"It is amazing, you're right. Inside me, your sperm are swimming up, searching for an egg to fertilize. It sounds so scientific for an act that was born out of pure emotion."

"Hey, there was science involved. I was quoting $E=mc^2$ in my head while I was going down on you."

We both start laughing, and she gets the giggles. She has a beautiful laugh—I don't hear it anywhere near enough.

"You have a lovely chuckle," she says, resting her hand on my chest and yawning. "It starts all the way down here. You don't laugh enough. You're so serious normally."

"I was just thinking the same about you."

"Maybe we just haven't found the right person to laugh with." She exhales, her breath fanning across my chest.

"Maybe."

She mumbles something I can't quite hear. It sounds like, "Fuck him."

"Pardon?" I ask, but she says, "Nothing."

Outside, the light above us flashes occasionally, sending its warning out to sea. But in here it's quiet and cozy. Poppy's body is warm and soft. Her hair smells of mint, and her skin of strawberries. Everything about this girl makes my mouth water.

In less than a minute, we're both asleep.

*

I'm a light sleeper, and I rouse a couple of times in the night, once to pee, and the second time I go down to the fridge and grab a bottle of water for a drink. Each time, when I come back to bed, Poppy's sleeping soundly. In the moonlight, her skin looks like porcelain, and her hair is a silvery gray. She looks so beautiful that I take a photo of her with my phone, captured in repose. God, she's so beautiful it makes my heart ache.

I think about her mumbled words, *Fuck him*. She was talking about Daniel. Maybe before she slept with me, she could tell herself he was normal, and sex was like that for everyone, but now? Perhaps I've done her a disservice, and she would have been better not knowing.

Then I think I might have made her pregnant, and my lips curve up a little. I slide back into bed and slip my arms around her, and she snuggles back against me. I'm not going to tell myself she would have been happier without this.

I fall asleep with my cheek resting on her hair, and I dream of mint and strawberries, and summer.

*

The next time I wake, the sky's the color of cinnamon, so I know it must be around six-thirty. I'm wrapped around Poppy, and she's fast asleep. I yawn and stretch, discover I have a hard-on, and decide it's a shame to waste it when I'm trying to get the girl pregnant.

I begin by moving aside her glorious hair to kiss her neck. The skin here is soft, and I press my lips behind her ear, and slowly down her neck to her shoulder. She stirs, but I don't stop, kissing her shoulder and upper arm.

"Marc?" she whispers.

"Go back to sleep." I push her gently onto her front. She shifts, burying her face in the pillow, and I push the duvet down, exposing her pale back. All that luscious skin, begging to be kissed. I press my lips down her spine, then either side of it, covering as much space as I can, taking my time to brush my lips over each rib and muscle, occasionally touching my tongue there, too. I kiss down her sides, reach her hips, and kiss over her bottom. I'm an ass man, and Poppy's is exemplary, so I take my time here, kissing the plump muscles, nibbling occasionally, and trailing my tongue up to her tailbone, which makes her shiver. I run my tongue along the crease of her bottom and down her thigh, part her legs, and bring up a hand to join in the fun.

I stroke down over her bottom and continue beneath her, just brushing lightly, not penetrating, not yet. She shivers again, and I smile, knowing I'm starting to get to her. She's no different from any other woman; all it takes is attention and time, like planting a seed and watching it grow. It's not rocket science.

Lying beside her, I continue to press my lips to her back and bottom while I stroke her, and then after a few minutes, I finally press my fingers a little firmer, and sink them into her folds. She's swollen and moist, and I sigh as I glide my middle finger to her clit. I circle my finger over the tiny button, and she moans and widens her legs, showing me how much she likes it.

"That's it," I murmur, keeping up a slow, steady rhythm. "Good girl. Just relax." I stretch out beside her, propping my head on my hand, and kiss her neck, her ear, and, when she turns her head to look at me with her wide green eyes, her mouth, as my fingers slip through her folds.

This time, she opens her mouth willingly for me, and when I tease her tongue with mine, she returns with small thrusts of her own. My blood begins to heat and pump faster around my body, and I feel an overwhelming urge to be inside her.

I wait, though, playing with her for as long as I can bear it. While I do, part of me observes that need with interest. The research I did on getting pregnant has made me think about how much of lovemaking is driven by a desire to procreate, and how what seems to be instinctive and impulsive is actually nature taking over, pulling the strings without us knowing. My body wants to inseminate her, regardless of what my brain thinks about it. For some reason, I have no idea why, it makes me hot.

I was going to bring her to orgasm and then arouse her again before I penetrated her, but I can't wait. I shift on the bed, moving up and between her legs. She gasps and stiffens, no doubt haunted by memories of the Maggot driving into her from behind without any thought to how it felt for her. I feel a fierce need to prove to her it doesn't need to be like that.

"I'm going to go slow," I murmur in her ear. "I can go deeper like this. Deeper inside you. Don't you think that would be nice?"

She tips her head to the side as I touch my tongue to her earlobe and her lips part in a soft moan. "Maybe."

"I'll be gentle. I'm here for you, remember? Do you trust me?"

She glances over her shoulder. "Yes," she whispers.

I kiss her lips. "I'm going to make you come again. And again, and again this week, in every position I can think of. Until all you can think about is me and how it feels to come with me inside you, filling you up."

She drops her forehead onto the pillow. "Marc…"

I push up her left knee and position myself beneath her, then press the tip of my erection against her entrance. Slowly, I push forward.

She groans, so I stop and withdraw, then do it again, coating myself with her moisture and going a tiny bit deeper with each thrust. It's hard to go slow; I want to plunge into her, bury myself inside her, but I clench my hands in the duvet and grab hold of all my willpower, forcing myself to take my time.

She's breathing heavily, so I stop and slide my hand beneath her. I cup her breast and brush over her nipple with my thumb, and as I kiss her neck, she exhales with a sigh.

"Just relax," I say softly, kissing up to her ear, because I know she likes that. I trace around the edge with my tongue and then blow softly. "Let me love you."

I slip my hand further down, beneath her, into her folds, and swirl a finger over her clit. I massage it for a while, giving small, shallow thrusts.

"Oh God." She relaxes her thighs and more moisture eases my way inside her, so I push forward, and this time I go all the way.

I pause and rest my forehead on her shoulder, reveling in the feeling of being enclosed in her warmth. "That feels so good," I tell her, beginning to move again, and continuing to circle my finger between her legs. "I like being inside you. Do you like it?"

"Yes," she whispers.

"Tell me you like it."

"I… like it."

"I like doing it like this," I tell her, feeling a little feverish. "Without a condom. Making you pregnant. Making you mine."

"Marc…"

"Tell me you want me to make you come."

"Oh God." Her teeth tug at her bottom lip and her brow creases. She's not far from coming, and I'm only seconds behind her.

"Tell me," I urge her, slowing my finger.

She groans with frustration. "Ohhh... I want you to make me come."

"Tell me you want me to come inside you."

"I... oh... want you to come inside me."

I stroke her more firmly, and she tips her head back. Her eyes are closed, her cheeks flushed, Jesus, she's so fucking beautiful like this. I can't help it; my hips speed up and I plunge inside her, but she doesn't seem to mind. She pushes back against me, her lips parting, and her hands curl where they clutch the pillow as she reaches out for her climax.

"Oh God," she says, "don't stop..."

"I'm not going to stop, honey." I kiss down her neck and suck gently where her pulse beats. "I'll take you all the way, remember?"

"Mmm... I'm so close..."

My fingers slide through her swollen folds, as I guide her closer to the edge. "There's no rush. I'll wait for you. I'm ready to fill you up when you're ready."

"Ah jeez... I... can't..."

"Yes you can. Stop reaching. Just let it happen. Let me guide you there. Let me lead."

She unfurls her hands, and a little of the tension leaves her body.

"That's it." I know she's close. I can feel her tightening, deep inside. I love this moment, knowing she's seconds away from bliss. "There it is, can you feel it coming? Let it take you."

"Marc..." She shudders and then cries out as she clenches around me. "Oh... fuck..." She clamps hard, and it's too much for me—there's no way I can hang on when she's doing that.

I thrust harder, and in less than ten seconds, my climax hits me. Heat rushes up from my balls, and I expel jet after jet inside her. Ah, Jesus, that feels good... such exquisite pleasure... accompanied by a smug satisfaction at the thought that I made her come. Oh yeah, fuck yeah... Poppy King, you're mine now, no other guy is ever going to touch you again.

Chapter Fourteen

Poppy

Marc is heavy on top of me, hard inside me. This moment is going to remain vivid in my memory forever, as if someone has opened the top of my skull and engraved a picture on my brain.

The rising sun fills the room with a warm orange glow. It's warm, too, although that's probably more to do with the amount of heat we're generating. I'm covered in sweat, and Marc's chest is sticking to my back.

I'm exhausted, physically and mentally. Last night, I'd wondered whether the sex we'd had was a one-off, born out of my naivety. It was a novelty, like nothing I'd experienced before, and I'd assumed subsequent times could never be as amazing.

Ohhh... silly, silly Poppy.

He's still inside me, and he moves now, giving a couple of small thrusts as he kisses my neck, and an aftershock of pleasure runs through me.

I give a little groan, and he chuckles. "Not nice?"

"You're squishing me," I tell him.

"So?"

"Marc..."

He nibbles my earlobe, still moving inside me. "Good morning."

I try not to laugh, and fail. "How come you're still hard? Does it ever go down?"

"Not when you're around." He sighs, withdraws, and shifts onto the bed beside me. As I go to get up, though, he pulls me back into his arms.

"I'm hot," I complain, "and I need to pee."

"Not yet. Let your uterus marinate in my little fellas for a few minutes."

I give in and lie back in his arms. He smells hot, of clean sheets, aftershave, and sex. It's strange that he's thinking about getting me pregnant while we make love. Odd that he knows so much about it. He's so quiet and broody, I hadn't expected him to be like this in bed. Confident and knowledgeable. Just thinking about his demand, *Tell me you want me to come inside you*, fills my face with heat.

"What?" he asks.

"Nothing."

He smirks. "Still think women can't have an orgasm during sex?"

"Don't be smug."

"Absolutely I'm going to be smug. I intend to prove it at least twice a day this week."

I blow out a breath. "The likelihood of getting pregnant doesn't increase the more times you do it in a day, as long as you do it around ovulation."

"So? I want you to get your money's worth."

Something in his voice makes me blink and frown. I thought I heard a touch of resentment in his words. But then I'm terrible at reading people, so maybe I'm hearing that wrong.

He leans forward and kisses me, so I guess he's not angry. He slides his tongue into my mouth, his hand moving down my back to my butt, and I shiver and say, "Stop it."

He laughs and rolls over, sitting up. "Come on then. We should have a shower and breakfast. Gotta keep your strength up." He smirks at me again over his shoulder and goes into the bathroom.

I lie on my back, lift my arms above my head, and look up at the ceiling. I feel pleasantly mellow and achy. Well-used. The thought makes me giggle. He's such a naughty boy. Telling me he'd only make a baby the old-fashioned way. *I get you, Poppy.* He wanted me, and I suppose he found a way to have me; he doesn't care it's only temporary. If I really liked a man, I wouldn't be satisfied with just sex. But that's guys for you.

I catch my bottom lip between my teeth. Am I using him, or is he using me? I suppose it's both. And we're both getting what we want out of it.

I don't want to think of it like that. It sounds cold and clinical, and I don't want it to be like that. This is fun, and at the end he'll get his money, he'll have satisfied his curiosity where I'm concerned, and I'll hopefully be pregnant. Everyone will be happy.

He sticks his head out of the door, his face half-covered in shaving foam. "Shower's hot."

My eyebrows rise. "What?"

"Seems a shame to waste the water. Come on." He disappears again.

He wants me to shower with him?

I think of that rock-hard body, his bulging biceps, all shiny from the water, and pull a pillow over my face. He's trying to kill me. I'm literally going to die from lust.

"Poppy!" he yells.

"All right. Keep your panties on." I get up, still grumbling, and go into the bathroom. Then I stop and stare at him. He's standing in front of the mirror, naked, halfway through shaving. It's such a masculine picture, I'm tempted to take a photo and turn it into a poster for my wall.

He glances at me as I enter and meets my eyes, the razor pausing on his cheek. "What?"

"Nothing." I swallow and glance at the toilet. "I need to pee."

"Don't let me stop you."

"I'm not peeing with you in the room."

He laughs and draws the razor up his throat. "After what we've just done?"

"Marc!"

He sighs and rinses the razor. "Hold on a sec." He finishes the last few strokes, splashes his face with cold water, and dries it on a towel as he goes out, giving me a wry look on the way.

I pee as quickly as I can, flush, then call him back in. He tosses the towel aside, takes my hand, and leads me into the shower cubicle. Ooh, it's tiny. We have to squidge up together so he can close the door.

The hot water pours over us, and the cubicle is filled with steam. Marc dips his head beneath the spray, soaking his hair. The water runs down his neck and over his chest. His muscles look like polished wood that's been out in the rain. He's soooo sexy.

He runs a hand through his hair, drawing it back off his face.

"It needs cutting," I tell him.

"I know. Can't be arsed." He turns so I'm under the shower. "Tip your head back."

I do as he says, letting the water soak my hair. He tips some shampoo onto his hand, then sinks it into my hair and gently massages it, his fingers grazing my scalp. Mmm, that feels good.

"I love your hair," he murmurs, smoothing his hands down the strands. "It's such a beautiful color."

"I hated it when I was younger," I say. "Nobody else in my family is ginger, and I always stood out like a sore thumb."

"Where does it come from, then? A grandparent?"

"Yes, Mom's mom, apparently, although she's gray now."

"You don't have any gray in yours," he says, rinsing the suds out.

"I do. A few strands. I'm getting old."

"Hardly," he scoffs. "Conditioner?"

"Please."

"Turn around."

I turn so my back is to him, and he pours some on his hands and smooths it through my hair. While he does it, he bends and places a kiss on my shoulder. Then another on my neck. I sigh.

"Don't worry," he says. "I won't do anything untoward."

"It wasn't a complaint."

"Glad to hear it." He reaches for the shower gel, pours some onto the puff, then places it on my shoulder. Slowly, he soaps me, washing down my back and over my hips. "Hands on the tiles," he instructs.

I lift my hands and lean on the tiles in front of me. He washes around my waist and up to my breasts, using slow circles, although he avoids my nipples. It doesn't matter though; it's still sensual, still sexy. It's the way he's looking at me, I think, his gaze following his hands, studying and admiring. He makes me glow.

"Turn back," he says eventually. I face him, and he proceeds to wash down me, sliding the puff between my legs with a sexy smile, then continuing down my thighs and calves before he straightens and hands me the puff. "Your turn."

Ooh, I get a turn? First, I wash his hair, smiling as it curls around my fingers, then I pour some more shower gel onto the puff, place it on his chest, and start washing him. All across his pecs, down to his abs, my fingers following, tracing the line of his muscles. By the time I get to his crotch, he has a slight erection. He gives me a shrug that says, *What are you gonna do?* I chuckle and wash around it, then twirl my finger in the air to ask him to turn. He rotates and leans on the glass. Now I get to do his back. I wash across his broad shoulders, over his shoulder blades, and down his spine. And then I stop.

I'd completely forgotten about his accident.

Running down the bottom of his spine like a zip is a long scar. Surgeons have cut into him here, and I remember him saying he has titanium plates screwed into the bone. There are another two scars on his right hip, deep scars, maybe where they took bone grafts, and a variety of other scars, turned a light pink with age.

"Oh, Marc," I say, running my fingers lightly over them.

"Quite the Frankenstein's monster," he replies, his head dipped.

"It's amazing," I tell him, breathless with wonder. "To think what they can do."

"I guess." He turns his head, although he doesn't meet my eyes.

"I'm so sorry you had to go through it. I wish I could have been there for you." I can't bear to think of the pain he must have been in. How difficult it must have been to get walking again.

I move up close to him, slide my arms around his waist, and rest my cheek on his back.

He lowers one hand and rests it over mine for a moment, and then he turns and wraps his arms around me. Surprised, I hug him tightly, sensing he needs the comfort, and we stay like that for a long time, the hot water pouring over us, steam curling up into the air. Eventually, he slides a hand under my chin, and lifts it so I'm looking into his eyes. Then he lowers his head and kisses me. It's a sweet kiss, just a press of his lips to mine, but for some reason my eyes prick with tears.

"Come here," he says, his husky voice suggesting he's not untouched by the moment. He turns me so I'm under the hot water again and rinses the conditioner out of my hair. Then he switches off the hot water, and we go out and dry ourselves off.

Marc doesn't speak again, and eventually he goes out and starts getting dressed. I stay in and comb my hair, studying my reflection while I do and thinking about how he held me. Something I said got to him. What did I say? *I'm so sorry you had to go through it. I wish I could have been there for you.* Maybe it made him think about Mel, and how things went wrong between them. It must have been so hard for him, having her pull away at the time he needed her the most.

It's the first time I've ever really thought about the "in sickness and in health" part of marriage vows, and it makes me think about my relationship with Daniel while I get ready. If you can call it a relationship. It's only now I realize what little depth it had. We led separate lives, and even though he left his wife for a while, it didn't really change anything between us. We were like strangers living in the same house while he stayed with me. There was no intimacy, no real affection. All along, I thought the problem was with me, but for the first time I think maybe it was Daniel who was the cold one. I think he left his wife because he could boast to his friends that he was dating a younger woman, and he thought it would be exciting, but in reality we didn't connect at all. Even though I've only had a few hours with Marc, I feel closer to him than I did with Daniel, who lived with me for six months. How strange. I just didn't realize at the time.

I put on some makeup, and by the time I go into the bedroom, Marc is dressed, the bed is made, and he's sitting back against the pillow, legs crossed at the ankles, reading on his phone.

He glances up as I come out and lowers the phone, but doesn't say anything. Instead, he watches me get dressed. A small smile plays on his lips as I pull on my panties and do up my bra. I don't say anything either, conscious he enjoys watching me. Instead, I pull on my jeans and sweater, then stand in front of the mirror and start drying my hair with the hairdryer.

I wonder if he still loves Mel, or if what she did destroyed any affection he had for her. The thought plays on my mind, and when I eventually finish my hair and start trying to wrangle it into a ponytail, I say to him, "Do you miss Mel?"

"Why do you ask that?"

I shrug, wrapping an elastic around the strands that fight hard to escape. "Just wondered."

He gets up then, comes over, turns me to face him, and slides his arms around me.

"No," he says, just the one word, very Marc. And then he kisses me again.

When he eventually pulls back, I say, "I didn't expect this while we were away."

He tucks a stray strand of hair behind my ear. "Expect what?"

"All this kissing."

He chuckles. "You don't like kissing?"

"I didn't say that. I thought we would be more... businesslike." I honestly thought we'd meet in the evenings, have sex, and that would be the extent of our connection.

He holds my chin and brushes his thumb across my bottom lip. "I'm very conscious of our arrangement," he says softly. "I know what you require from me, and I'm happy to supply it. The kissing's extra."

He gives me an amused look, bends and picks up his phone, and leaves the room.

I pout and pick up my purse. *The kissing's extra.* I should have written out a contract and gotten him to sign it, forcing him to stick to the terms.

Chapter Fifteen

Fitz

We eat our breakfast outside, sipping our coffee while seagulls swoop overhead and the sea crashes on the rocks.

Poppy sits under an umbrella, presumably worried about catching the sun. I'm wearing sunglasses, so I'm able to study her without her knowing. She reads off her phone while she crunches her toast, scooping up loose crumbs off her lip with her finger into her mouth. Her hair is struggling to remain bound by the elastic, and loose strands lift around her face in the early morning breeze.

I'm tempted to take the band from her hair, strip off all her clothes, and make love to her out here, on the patch of grass around the lighthouse. I can't believe I'm hot for her again when it's been less than an hour since we've had sex. But I am. I don't know why I find her so sexy. I think maybe it's her naivety, the way she's surprised by everything I do. It's as if I've taken her to Disneyland, and she's walking around permanently dazed by all the bright lights and colors.

"Stop staring at me," she says without looking up.

"How can you tell? I'm wearing sunglasses."

"I can feel your eyes on me like lasers."

I chuckle and return my gaze to my phone. "Sorry. You look luscious sitting there, that's all."

"Hardly," she says, running a hand over her hair. "It's gone all flyaway this morning. I should have braided it."

I pull up a picture on my phone of Jack wearing a wig with ginger braids, and show it to her. "Like this?"

She bursts out laughing. "Oh my God, poor Jack! Did you do that to him?"

"It was Halloween. He wanted to join in."

"Aw, the poor pup. Are you missing him?"

"I am, actually. It's funny not having him under my feet all the time. Mind you, I've been a bit busy to notice."

She gives me a wry look and returns to her phone. "Not my fault if you can't keep it in your pants."

"You can't blame it. It's like a lion that's escaped from the zoo after years of captivity."

She laughs, and I smile. My work here is done.

"Shall we get going soon?" I ask her, and she nods and finishes off her toast.

"I'll drop you off," she says, "and then I'm heading over to the petting farm on the other side of Hastings. I'll be back mid-afternoon, probably."

"Okay."

We take the breakfast things in and wash up, gather our stuff, and go to the car. Soon we're heading toward the Ark.

Poppy's driving today, which gives me free rein to look out of the window and admire the landscape. It's almost as beautiful as in the Bay of Islands—almost, but not quite. Although I spent a few years here, I much prefer it up in the bay. I suppose memories of that time don't help.

"Penny for them," Poppy says.

I sigh. "I was thinking about last time I was in Hawke's Bay."

"About Mel?"

"Yes and no. I remember it as being a dark time, despite the fact that I was engaged to Mel. The more I think about it, the more I'm not surprised she canceled the wedding. I was so angry during that time. Not at her, but resentful that my career had been cut short, and frustrated that I'd lost my physicality. It was important to me at the time—all the sport. I used to run for an hour every morning."

"That's keen."

"Yeah. I was pretty fit."

"You still are," Poppy says. "You keep yourself in good shape. Do you still run?"

I like her throwaway compliment. "Yes, but slower, and not for as long. And I do weights to keep the muscle tone up. It's not the same though."

"No, I get that. But then you wouldn't have been able to maintain that level of fitness into your thirties, I wouldn't have thought. As we age, we become more prone to injuries, less bouncy. It takes more work to keep up that level of fitness."

"Yeah."

"Do you resent getting older?" she asks. "Are you going to buy a red sports car and have affairs with women half your age when you get into your forties?"

That makes me laugh. "I don't think so. I guess I just thought I'd be somewhere different by now."

She glances over at me. "Married and with kids?"

"Maybe. And perhaps a captain or a major in the Army, eventually. I'd have liked that."

"I can call you sir, if it would help."

I glance over at her. She raises her eyebrows.

"Don't tempt me," I tell her.

She smiles. "For what it's worth, I'm glad you came out of the Army. I wouldn't have met you otherwise. And then we wouldn't be having all this fun."

"I'm glad you're enjoying yourself." For a fleeting moment, I think about the fact that, if all goes according to plan, she'll be pregnant, and then the fun will be over. But what's the point in worrying about tomorrow and not enjoying today? Carpe Diem, Fitz.

She takes the turnoff for the Ark and stops outside the main building. "Okay," she says, "I'll see you later."

"Sure." I hesitate and meet her green eyes. I want to lean forward and kiss her. But she's not my wife, and she's not my girlfriend. I don't know what she is. The thought makes me uncomfortable. But there's nothing I can do about it, so I give her a brief smile, then get out of the car and watch her drive away.

I shove my hands into the pockets of my jeans, put her out of my mind, and go into the main building.

*

I'm relatively successful at not thinking about her for a good part of the day. Ashton keeps me busy, and there's lots to do. In the morning, we walk around the site, talking about the plans for the rest of the buildings, and I tell him about some of the issues we had with drainage runoff and laying pipes, and how we overcame those problems. We go over the plans together, spreading them out in his brand-new conference room, on the floor because he doesn't have any furniture yet. And we talk about sourcing materials and building contractors, amenities, and the cost of actually getting the place up and running. Ashton's around my age and we get on well, so the morning passes quickly.

By one o'clock, we're both ready for a break. We order a beer and a sandwich at a bar five minutes down the road and sit outside, in the shade. We're not far from the river, and as the waitress delivers our food, a Labrador comes bounding past us, soaked through where he's obviously been for a swim.

"That's Sandy," Ashton explains. "He belongs to Terry, the bartender. He's always in the river."

I chuckle. "My Jack Russell hates water. When it's bath time, he makes a right fuss."

Ashton grins and has a long swallow of his beer, then takes a bite of his sandwich. "Terry's wife jokes that Sandy's half dog, half dolphin. I've seen the dog leap into the water from the bank. Mel gives him scores as if he's in the Olympics."

My heart judders to a stop. I have a mouthful of sandwich, and for a moment I'm worried I'm going to choke. I take a sip of beer and force myself to chew a few more times before I swallow. "Mel?" I ask as casually as I can.

"Yeah," Ashton replies. "Do you know her?"

"I don't know, possibly." We used to live in Napier, but Hastings isn't far away, so it's not beyond the realms of possibility that she moved here. There must be lots of Mels in Hawke's Bay, though. "What's her name short for?" I cross my fingers that he'll say Melanie.

"Carmella, I think," Ashton says. "Unusual, isn't it? Like in *The Sopranos*, although I don't think she's Italian."

"How long have they been married?" My hand is shaking, and I cover it by having a swig of beer.

"Not sure, four, five years? They've got a couple of kids, and the oldest is about four, I think. How do you know her?"

"Oh, we were friends a long time ago." I want to leave, but I can't without it looking weird. I force myself to eat my sandwich. I didn't see her in the bar when we went in to order, so she's probably out. "Anyway," I say to change the subject, "I wonder how Poppy's getting on at the petting farm?"

"Yeah, I'm looking forward to having a chat to her this afternoon," Ashton replies. "She obviously knows her stuff. She's pretty gorgeous, too. I was thinking about asking her out for a drink tonight."

For the second time in as many minutes, my heart skips a beat. I feel a stab of jealousy at the thought of him taking her out, and have to stop myself giving him a right hook.

Ashton looks at me, sees my glare, and looks startled. "Oh, shit. Are you and she… you know…?"

"Not officially but, yeah, kinda."

"Crap. I'm so sorry."

I push my jealousy away. How was he supposed to know? "It's not your fault. We're flying under the radar, so to speak. Nobody knows."

"Well, you're a lucky man." He clears his throat. "Did you see the All Blacks game last Saturday?"

Relieved he's changed the subject, I nod, and we start talking about the lineup, and what it means for the upcoming game against the Aussies next month.

I scold myself, though, for acting like a caveman. Poppy isn't mine, and I don't have the right to act as if I own her.

And yet… we are sleeping together. I'm trying to get her pregnant. Doesn't that give me any rights?

Maybe, maybe not.

"Just gonna visit the Gents'," Ashton says, and he disappears inside. I push the rest of the sandwich away, and finish off my beer. I want to get back to the Ark. I feel uncomfortable here, out of place, out of time. I miss the bay, the comfort of our own Ark, the Kings and the others I work with, and Jack, who's always at my side. And I wish Poppy was here with me.

"Fitz?"

I freeze, then turn slowly at the woman's voice. Mel's standing in the doorway to the bar, shading her eyes with her hand. Her other hand rests on her very pregnant bump. She's two years older than me, so she must be thirty-four now. Despite the bump, she's lost quite a lot of weight, and her face is gaunt. She's also cut her hair; the long blonde locks are gone, replaced with a short bob. I don't like her new look. It makes her look beautiful but hard.

"Hey, Mel." I stand reluctantly as she approaches and slide my hands into the pockets of my jeans.

"What are you doing here?" She doesn't look upset or angry, just curious.

"I'm visiting the animal sanctuary up the road."

"The Ark? Oh, are you involved in that?"

"I help run its sister Ark in the Bay of Islands."

"So that's where you ended up," she says softly. "You vanished off the face of the Earth."

I don't reply. It's hard, seeing her again. I'd wondered whether this would ever happen, and how I'd react. I thought I might get angry or upset, but I just feel numb.

"How long are you here for?" she asks.

"Not long."

"What's life like in the bay?"

"Great."

"Effusive as ever," she says, a touch of sarcasm in her voice.

I don't want to be rude, but I don't want to talk to her. It twists me up inside. I used to love this woman. I thought we had a future together. But she turned her back on me when I needed her most, and she walked away.

I don't want to congratulate her on her marriage and her kids. On being pregnant. On having a wonderful life without me. Fuck her. She hurt me, and I'm not over it. I thought I was, but maybe the wound she gave me will never heal the way my back has. It's buried deep within me like shrapnel, slicing through me whenever I think it's gone.

"How's your back?" she asks.

"Do you care?" I snap.

She studies my face. "I wouldn't have asked if I didn't."

"It's fine," I tell her. "Thanks for your concern."

Her brow furrows. "Don't be like that."

"It's difficult not to be, Mel, when you left me because of the injury. It's a bit hypocritical to be asking about it now, don't you think?"

"I didn't leave you because of your injury," she says.

"Oh, yeah, right. You left because it 'changed me.'" I put sarcastic air quotes around the words. "As if I was expected to come through it all unscathed."

"I left because you didn't want me anymore," she replies, a glimmer of tears in her eyes.

I glare at her. "What are you talking about?"

"You shut yourself off from me after the accident. You withdrew completely. You wouldn't talk to me about it, about anything, in fact." She's gone pale. "I wanted to help you; I could see you were in pain, but I felt so alone. I was scared of marrying you when I wasn't sure if we could go back to the way things were."

"You hardly gave us time to find out," I say harshly, my stomach churning.

"I know." She bites her lip. "I met Terry, and I fell in love with him. He's an open book, and it was so refreshing after being with you. You have padlock after padlock around your heart Fitz—you always did have, even before the accident. You said you loved me, but you always kept a large piece of yourself hidden from me."

"I don't even know what that means. I never kept any secrets from you."

"I don't mean secrets. I mean your feelings, what was in your heart."

"So I don't go around blurting out my emotions. Sue me!"

I'm aware that I'm raising my voice to a pregnant woman, and I force myself to lower it, to calm down. This is a pointless conversation. I don't know what she's trying to say, and she doesn't understand that I didn't make any conscious effort to keep anything from her. I don't feel the need to discuss every thought that goes through my head. That's just who I am. Poppy seems to understand that. Why didn't Mel?

"I don't want to argue," she says. "I just wanted to say hi."

"Well, you've said it." Ashton comes out, so I say, "Good luck with the baby. Gotta go now."

"Hey, Mel," Ashton says, coming over to kiss her cheek. "You're looking well."

"Thanks." She looks a bit upset and glances my way, but I turn and walk off, back to the car.

I'm breathing heavily, struggling to contain my emotion. I wish Poppy was here, with her mad hair and her calm manner. I think of the way she stood behind me in the shower this morning and slid her arms around me. She didn't have to say anything; that brief touch demonstrated her sympathy, and her affection for me.

I wish she was mine. I wish I had someone of my own. I'm lonely, and bitter, and I don't want to continue living that way. But Poppy's not looking for a companion. I think I'm destined to be lonely and bitter for the rest of my life.

Clouds are moving over the sun, promising rain. Carpe diem, Fitz. Forget about anything else.

Chapter Sixteen

Poppy

I arrive back at the Ark mid-afternoon. I park out front, walk past the half-built veterinary center, cross to the new office building, and go inside. It smells of paint and varnish—the smell of promise and excitement. Or is it just me, looking forward to seeing Marc again?

"Hey," Ashton calls out as I pass the meeting room, and I stop in the doorway.

"Hi." I lift up the tray of takeaway coffees in my hand. "I called in at the Riverbank on the way past."

"Excellent. We were just ready for a break."

I go into the room and see Marc sitting on the floor, his back to the wall. Papers and plans lie all over the carpet in front of him, some covered in his neat, round handwriting. He looks up as I walk in, his eyes meeting mine, and I feel an electric shock hit me and run all the way down my body.

I go over, sit beside him, and pass him a coffee.

"Thanks," he says. He gives a smile, but it's half-hearted, and he drops his gaze afterward. If I didn't know better, I'd say he was upset about something.

"I'm just going to check on the delivery of the building materials that's coming this afternoon," Ashton says. "I won't be long and then you can tell me all about your petting farm." He takes his coffee and leaves the room.

I lean back against the wall and sip my coffee. "How are you doing?" I ask Marc. "Got much done?"

"Yeah, quite a lot actually. It's been a busy morning. You?"

I nod. "I had great fun. Found a petting farm and spent the morning with the woman who runs it. I picked up quite a few tips."

"Great." He smiles, then swigs his coffee.

"You okay?" I ask. "Something on your mind?"

He gives me a curious look. "I thought you said you weren't any good at reading people?"

"I'm not, normally. But you seem… I don't know. Sad."

He drops his gaze back to his coffee cup and sighs. "I bumped into Mel."

My jaw drops. "Oh no. Where?"

"At the Riverbank. You might have seen her if you went in there for the coffees. Blonde. Pregnant."

"She served me." Holy shit, that was his ex? Ouch, the bump must have been painful to see. Oddly, she didn't look like what I expected. It's funny how you always imagine other women to be younger and prettier than yourself.

"Ashton says she has two kids already," he says.

"I'm sorry." I reach out and take his hand.

He curls his fingers around mine, looking at them as if surprised to see them there. "It was a shock, that's all," he says softly.

"Of course it was."

"I didn't expect to see her."

"No, why would you? I'm not surprised it shook you up a bit." I squeeze his fingers. "But you've moved on now, eh? New job, new life. You deserve better than her, Marc."

He meets my gaze. There's a strange expression on his face, although I can't decipher it this time. Then, to my surprise, he lifts a hand to cup the back of my head and pulls me toward him for a kiss.

Conscious that Ashton could walk in, I feel my face warm, but I don't want Marc to think I'm not interested in kissing him, so I close my eyes and give in. I know the kiss is connected with him seeing Mel—maybe he's proving to himself that he's still attractive to women, or probably more that he needs comfort after seeing she's moved on. Either way, I'm happy to help, and I touch my tongue to his bottom lip, following which he slides his tongue against mine, and we indulge in a long, sensual, somewhat erotic kiss that leaves me tingling all over.

When he eventually moves back, I press my lips together and lean against the wall. "Mmm," I say. "Yum."

He gives a short laugh and swigs his coffee. "Yeah," he says, "that about sums it up."

Ashton comes back in at that moment, bringing an end to the conversation, but it takes a while for me to stop tingling.

He declares there are some other members of the Ark arriving outside, keen to meet us, so we wander out into the blustery afternoon and shake hands with the two men—Ken and Hemi, and one woman—Sally, who are founding members of the new sanctuary. Furniture is in short supply, but someone has some fold-up chairs in their car, and soon we're all sitting on the grass, talking about Noah's Ark and discussing similarities and differences.

Sally asks me about the success of the petting farm, and I start telling them about it. I list a few of the studies Leon quoted in his visit to the Beehive when he did his presentation to the Prime Minister, explaining how we're hoping that teaching children to respect animals at an early age might improve the number of incidents of violence in the family home.

"I give a little talk at the beginning of each tour," I tell them, "explaining about how the animals aren't stuffed toys or cartoon characters—that they're like people, and have feelings and emotions, and that pets especially rely on us to take care of them. It's surprising how many children… er…"

My voice trails off as my gaze falls on Marc. He's watching me, and as I meet his eyes, I find his filled with a sultry desire. He's thinking about me naked. About sex. Specifically, having sex with me. Oh. That's thrown me. What was I saying?

He lifts an eyebrow, and I tear my gaze away, clear my throat, and carry on. "Yes, um, it's surprising how many children don't think about the animal in that way." I continue talking, keeping my gaze averted from him so he can't distract me, but inside I have butterflies, and my heart is racing.

The conversation continues for a while, moving on to the veterinary center, and as Hemi and Ashton tell us about their plans for creating a Ward Seven the same as at Noah's Ark, my gaze drifts back to Marc. He's listening to them, nodding, and adding something every now and then, but at that point he meets my gaze for a second time. He doesn't smile, but it's like an electric shock to my system again. How can he do that with just a look?

We stay at the Ark for another hour, but even though I join the others in a wander around the site, and I listen to the conversation, my mind isn't on it. I keep thinking about that morning, when Marc woke me by kissing my back before sliding into me from behind, and how he so easily, so effortlessly, coaxed me to a climax again. I want more of that. I'm hungry for him. I'm a little tender down below—Jesus, what a surprise, after having sex twice within twelve hours—but still, I want him again. Will he want to have sex with me later? Definitely, if that hot look in his eyes is anything to go by.

Ashton stops by the fence around one of the paddocks to talk about the possible site for their own petting farm, and when I lean on the fence, Marc comes and leans beside me. He's not touching me; his arm is half an inch away from mine. But I can feel him with every fiber of my being. I can almost smell his skin, feel his muscles beneath my fingers. I want to slide my hand beneath his T-shirt onto his back; trace his spine up to his shoulder blades. I want to feel his mouth on mine. I want him inside me.

"Poppy?"

I jump at Sally's voice behind me and turn. "Sorry?"

"I just asked whether you both wanted to join us for dinner tonight? We're all meeting up in town at a Chinese restaurant."

I glance at Marc. "Sure," he says. "But we might go back to the lighthouse first to catch up on a few phone calls and then get changed."

"Oh, you're staying at the lighthouse?" Sally says. "It's a lovely little cottage, isn't it? So picturesque."

"Yeah," he says, "I got a last-minute booking due to a cancellation. What time are you meeting?"

"Six-thirty, at the Golden Dragon."

"Okay, we'll meet you there. Poppy? Shall we shoot off?"

I nod, and we wave goodbye to the others and head back to the car.

He glances at me as we walk. "Why are you blushing?"

"You told them we're staying at the lighthouse."

"Yeah, so?"

"It only has one bedroom."

"Yeah…"

"So they all know we're staying together," I point out with some exasperation.

"Of course they do. I told Ashton we were an item."

That surprises me. "Did you?"

We arrive at the car, and get inside. "Yeah," Marc says, buckling in his seat belt and starting the engine. "He told me he was thinking of asking you out for a drink this evening."

"Oh!"

"I might have gotten a bit jealous and glared at him." He turns the car around and heads off down the road. "He asked if we were together and I cleared it up by saying 'not officially, but yeah, kinda.'" He gives me an amused look.

My head's whirling, and I feel a mixture of emotions.

"Sorry," he says. "Did I overstep the boundary?"

"No, it's okay."

"Did you want to go out for a drink with Ashton?"

I roll my eyes. "Of course not. I mean, I'm flattered he's interested, of course, but I'm not interested in him."

"Aren't you?"

"No."

He turns his hot gaze to me. "Good. Because when we get in, I'm going to screw you senseless."

Heat rushes through me, and I inhale sharply. "Marc!"

"What? Tell me you haven't been thinking about it all afternoon."

I can't deny it. "We're going out at six-thirty."

"It's not even five o'clock yet. Plenty of time for some afternoon delight."

My heart's hammering against my ribs. I want him, desperately, but equally I'm sure this is about Mel, and that gives me a funny twist in my stomach.

"You said you ovulate tomorrow," he reminds me when I don't say anything. "Might as well get as many of those swimmers trying to cross the channel as possible." He smirks as he takes the turnoff for the lighthouse.

I bite my lip as he navigates the narrow lane, and when he eventually pulls up and parks, he turns to me and tips his head to the side. "What?"

"Is this about Mel?" I ask softly. "Because I told you, we don't have to have sex all the time to get pregnant."

He looks into my eyes, then looks away, across the ocean. I follow his gaze. The blustery breeze is whipping the sea into peaks and troughs, and the spray coats the rocks with white lace.

"It's not about Mel," he says eventually, his gaze coming back to me. "Or at least, seeing her made me realize how special you are. In the few days we've been... intimate, I feel that you care for me more than she ever did."

My jaw drops; I'm incredibly touched by his words.

"I'm not saying I expect anything when this is over," he adds quickly. "I know this is a temporary arrangement."

"It's okay." I reach up a hand and cup his face. "I understand." I feel anger toward the cold woman who turned her back on him when he was so vulnerable. I want to make him feel better. To prove to him that he is worthy of love and affection.

I unbuckle my seat belt, shift closer to him, and pull his head down until his lips touch mine.

Mmm, I've been thinking about this all day. He smells so good. His lips move gently across mine, and then his tongue brushes my lip, and we exchange a deep, sensual kiss.

Ooh, it takes all of ten seconds for the tingles to pass through me, and already my nipples are tightening and I feel answering tremors deep inside. I want him, and it's obvious he wants me. His fingers are tightening in my hair, and when he tilts his head to slant his lips across mine, the kiss turns hot and demanding.

I push myself up to see if I can sit astride him, attempt to straddle him, and promptly sit on the horn in the middle of the steering wheel. The resulting blare makes us both jump, then laugh.

"Indoors," he instructs, lowering me back to his side. "I'm far too old and too big to have sex in a car, and besides, I can't go down on you like this." I shiver as he slips his hands beneath my sweater onto my skin and slides them up my back. "I want to taste you," he murmurs, pressing his lips to my neck. "I want to make you come with my mouth."

"I guess it's a shame to pass up on the chance to increase the amount of semen," I say, breathless.

He gives a short laugh. "Absolutely." He covers the place on my neck where my pulse is racing and sucks gently, and I groan.

"Right," he says, moving back. "Inside, now."

Chapter Seventeen

Fitz

I unlock the lighthouse door, grab Poppy's hand, and lead her inside. I'm kissing her before I've even locked the door. She got me so fired up in the car, if she hadn't sat on the horn, I might well have attempted to get her jeans off and have her on my lap.

But this makes more sense. I'm ready for her now, but I'm going to have to wait. I have lots of pleasuring to do first.

I pull her toward me, push her jacket off her shoulders, and toss it onto the sofa. Then I take her sweater by the hem and start pulling it up her body.

"Don't you want a drink first?" she asks faintly.

"Nope."

She sighs and lifts her arms, and I draw the sweater over her head and toss it on top of her jacket. Then I kiss her again, wrapping my arms around her.

She slips her hands beneath the hem of my T-shirt, and I shiver as she traces her fingers up my back to my shoulder blades. Her mouth is eager, her tongue sliding against mine, her kisses hot, demanding rather than asking, which fires me up. This is what I want—I want her to realize that it's acceptable to concentrate on her own pleasure.

I unclip her bra at the back, draw the straps down her arms, and let that drop. Then, still kissing her, I fill my palms with her breasts. The nipples are soft and velvety, and I tease the ends with my thumbs until they harden to beads, making her moan. The first time we slept together, she almost flinched when I touched her breasts, and I have a feeling her previous lovers have been too rough with her, so I made sure I was gentle; now, though, when I tug her nipples gently, she squirms against me and sinks her hands into my hair.

Moving back, I take her hand and lead her up the stairs to the bedroom. Once there, I gesture to her jeans while I unbutton mine, and we both remove them. Immediately, her hands are on the hem of my tee, and she drags it up my body and over my head before dropping it to the floor.

"Yes," she says, her voice husky, splaying her hands on my chest. "You have such an amazing body, Marc." She smooths her hands across my muscles, brushing her thumbs over my nipples.

"Thank you." I know I'm nothing special, but her compliment warms me.

"Look at your arms." She brings her hands over my shoulders and down to my biceps. "They're so hard."

I chuckle. "That's 'coz I'm a fella."

"No, I was right, you are a fine specimen."

"Are you trying to make me blush?" I maneuver her backward, toward the bed.

"I like that you work with your hands sometimes. You're intelligent and yet you also know how to fix a fence. It's a perfect combination."

"Glad I can be of service." I push her back so she falls onto the bed. "Move up."

She shuffles up the bed until her head is on the pillow, and I follow her on, kneeling between her legs. I hook my fingers into the elastic of her panties, draw them down her thighs, and remove them, then lean over her and look into her eyes.

"Hello," she says.

"Hello." I bend and kiss her. "Do you have any idea how crazy you make me?"

"A little." She lifts a knee and gently rubs it against my erection in the boxers.

I lie on top of her and kiss her, and when she wraps her legs around my waist, I rock my hips, stroking my erection through her folds, and she groans.

"That's it," I state, moving back and starting to kiss down her body. "I can't wait any longer." I stop to trace around her nipples with my tongue and suck them gently, then continue down, until I'm lying between her thighs. She covers her face with her hands as I push her thighs apart, exposing her to my gaze, and I bend my head and inhale her sweet, musky smell and sigh.

"Argh. Marc!"

SERENITY WOODS

"You smell amazing. I'm going to give you an orgasm with my mouth now. Just so you know." I give a long, slow lick through her folds.

"Mmm…" She sighs.

Smiling, I part her with my hands, then begin to tease her with my tongue and fingers. She's already on the way to being aroused, but within five minutes her folds are swollen and my fingers are covered with her moisture. All I've done is focus on licking her clit while I stroke her, but she's sunk one hand into my hair, and her breathing has deepened as she fills the air with her sighs.

For the first time, I slide two fingers deep inside her, curve them up, find the small swelling on the front wall of her vagina, and massage it gently while I continue to lick her. She moans and rocks her hips, and I know it's not going to be long before she comes. This time I'm going to take her all the way, but I want it to be good, so I slow the movement of my fingers and lick her slowly, sliding my tongue down through her folds before returning to circle it over her clit.

"Oh God," she whispers, "Marc…"

"Slowly," I murmur. "Just let it happen." Her clit is a hard button on my tongue, and I cover it with my mouth and suck gently as I carry on stroking inside her.

"Oh…" Her hands tighten in my hair. "I can't… I'm going to…"

I suck harder, and she cries out and comes, tightening around my fingers, pulsing and clenching. I wait for her to finish, enjoying every second of her pleasure, and when she finally collapses back on the pillow, I withdraw my fingers, satisfied.

I don't stop kissing and touching her, though. I stroke her thighs, kiss up over her belly, and take my time to reach her breasts before I start paying them attention again. Poppy sighs, tracing her hand over my back as I rest beside her and kiss her nipples, and when I eventually get to her mouth and kiss her, she sinks her hand into my hair and happily returns each thrust of my tongue with one of her own.

"Mmm," she murmurs. "That felt so good."

"That was just a starter," I tell her, rolling onto my back and pulling her toward me. "Now it's time for round two."

*

Poppy

Marc's relentless, still touching me, kissing me. My body is in a heightened state of arousal, and everything feels sensitive, as if he'd only have to breathe on me and I'd come again. I can't believe it. I didn't know it was possible to feel like this.

He leaves me for a second to rid himself of his boxers, then pulls me on top of him, pushing me up so I'm sitting astride him.

"You want me to be on top?" I ask.

"I do." The tip of his erection presses against my folds. "It's your turn to do the hard work."

"What do you mean?"

"I want you to ride me," he says. His eyelids have fallen to half-mast, and his expression is sultry, full of desire. "I want you to take your pleasure from me."

I'm not quite sure what he means, but I move back until he enters me, then sink down onto him. Ohhh… we both groan at the sensation of him being inside me. I rock my hips so he slides in and out. "Mmm."

"That's it," he says. Taking my right hand, he moves it down between my legs, then takes my other hand and moves it to my breast. "I want you to touch yourself the way you do when you're alone. You're going to make yourself come for me."

Heat fills my face. I've never done that with a man. I move both hands onto his chest. "I can't do that."

He lifts his hands above his head and wraps his fingers around the slats of the headboard, giving me one of his sexy smiles. "Use me, Poppy. Come on. Show me that you understand your pleasure is yours to give and take."

I swallow hard. The way he's lying, he looks as if he's tied up. Ooh. Now there's a fantasy I could get on board with.

"Tell me what you're thinking," he demands.

"You look as if you're tied up," I whisper.

"You like that idea?"

I moisten my lips with the tip of my tongue and begin to move on top of him. "Yes."

"You'd like to tie my hands up?"

"Yes."

"Keep me as your prisoner?" His lips curve up a little. He likes role-playing. I've never done it before, but his sultry eyes, his obvious desire, give me courage.

"Yes," I whisper, lowering a hand between us. I slide my fingers down, until I find my clit, and circle a finger over it. I feel exposed and vulnerable doing this in front of him, but his lips part and he swells inside me, and I can see it turns him on. "I'd like to chain you to my bed at home," I tell him. "So you're there for me at the end of the day."

"Waiting for you," he says. "Just for you. Like a sex slave."

"Mmm." Wow, what an amazing thought.

"Tell me what you'd do with me," he says.

I moisten my lips again. "I'd come into the room, and I'd tell you it was time for me to... use you. Would you beg me to let you go?"

"No." His voice is husky now. "I'd have been waiting all day for that moment. I'd have been hard all day."

I close my eyes briefly, concentrating on the feel of him, so thick and hard inside me. When I push down, I can feel him stretching me erotically, ohhh... that's so good... My finger swirls faster over my clit as I continue rocking my hips, forcing him to slide in and out.

"How would you use me?" he murmurs. "Describe how."

"Like this." I look down at where our bodies meet. "I'd climb on top of you and take you inside me. Or maybe I'd torture you a little with my mouth first." I haven't done that yet, but the thought of going down on him excites me.

For the first time, it looks as if his self-control is slipping. "Hmm," he says, closing his eyes for a moment. "You'd like that?"

"I would. I'd like to taste you, Marc. But obviously, I couldn't let you come in my mouth because you need to come inside me. I'd tell you off if you let yourself climax."

He opens his eyes again, his expression somewhat wry. "Would you now?"

"I would." I'm getting in the swing of it. I love this. Love that he's encouraging me to play. He really likes giving me pleasure. He wants me to come before him, so he can make sure I've enjoyed it. He wants me to accept that I'm entitled to my own pleasure, and that I can request it from him before he takes his from me.

"Show me how you'd use me," he says.

I begin to thrust harder, and, somewhat shyly, I lift my other hand to my breast and tease the nipple. It's weird to do this with a man watching, but his gaze is so hot it turns me on, and I pluck it harder as the fingers of my right hand slip through my folds. "Like this," I whisper, knowing I'm not far from coming again.

"You'd fuck me," he says. "Purely for your own enjoyment."

He loves to shock me. "Yes. You're just here to serve me." I suck my bottom lip. "Mmm…"

"Aaahhh…" He's struggling to stay calm now. "You feel so good."

"I don't care," I tell him, "you're going to wait."

His lips curve up, even as he groans. "Yes, ma'am."

Oh that's hot. "Just… wait… until… I'm ready…" I close my eyes. Pleasure is building deep inside me. I can't believe I'm doing this—using this man, taking him like this and concentrating only on my own desire. I tighten inside at the erotic thought, and then I come, clamping around him, my fingers stilling as the pulses take my breath away, five, six, seven times. It's such a beautiful feeling, made all the more wonderful by the gorgeous guy spread beneath me.

When I eventually stop, I lean on his chest and gasp, looking into his eyes. "Mm," I say.

He groans and moves his hips beneath me. "Can I come now, ma'am?"

I lick my lips and think about it for a moment. "Maybe. Have you been good?"

He blows out a breath and gives me a helpless look.

"I think I will make you come now," I tell him as I start moving again, "because I want you to fill me up."

He closes his eyes, his brow furrowing. "I'll do my best."

I bend and kiss him, dipping my tongue into his mouth. "Mmm… yes… come for me, I want to give you pleasure, I want to make you feel good…"

He lets go of the headboard and drops his arms to stroke down my back, then holds my hips for the final few thrusts before he buries himself deep inside me. I watch him, loving being able to see each spasm of pleasure on his face, and I capture his groans as I close my mouth over his and kiss him.

Oh God, I think that was the sexiest thing I've ever done. This guy is going to drive me insane with lust. He's trying to turn me into a nymphomaniac. I'm never going to be the same again.

Chapter Eighteen

Poppy

By six-thirty, we're at the Golden Dragon, meeting the gang at the Ark for a Chinese meal. Hemi and Sally have brought their partners, and the eight of us order a set meal and a round of Tiger beer to go with it.

Marc sits beside me, and he's quiet for a while, listening but not really joining in with the conversation. I glance at him, wondering whether it's to do with what happened in the bedroom. He'd looked as if he was enjoying it, but maybe he'd expected me to act in a different way, and I'd surprised or upset him. I can never tell.

He smiles at me, though, and he nudges my knee with his beneath the table, so I think he's okay.

It's odd being with people and the two of us being together, but not together. I want to lean against him, to have him put his arm around me, to show my affection for him, the way Sally is kissing her husband on the cheek in front of everyone. But I can't. It strikes me then what a bizarre agreement we have. It's almost like the scenario we enacted in the bedroom. He's servicing me, trying to get me pregnant. I'm treating him like a living, breathing sperm bank. He agreed to it, and I'm paying him for it, but maybe he's more upset about the arrangement than I thought.

I feel a tad resentful. It wasn't my idea to sleep together. I told him I wouldn't be interested in a relationship at the end. And I'm still not. I like him—of course I do, more than I thought I would. And it's not because he gives me multiple orgasms. Okay, it's not *just* because he gives me multiple orgasms. He's tender and gentle, although I'm beginning to realize he has a wicked streak hidden beneath that. He hid it well, no doubt because he thought it would be too much for me, but

I have a feeling that, given time and opportunity, Marc Fitzgerald could be a very naughty boy.

I shift in the chair, trying not to think about our adventure in bed that afternoon. I can't let myself get distracted. Because if I think about it—if I really think about having a relationship with him, about going to bed with him every night, about letting him do all those things to me on a regular basis, and more—I'm going to fall for him, and that'll be akin to taking a saw to my ribcage and opening up my ribs to give him access to my squidgy heart. I don't want to do that. I don't want to give someone that kind of power over me again.

No, this is just about sex. About getting pregnant, and nothing more. And if he's upset about it, well, he should have done something in a cup, as he so delicately put it.

The meal arrives—numerous wonderful dishes of noodles and rice, sticky chicken and Szechuan beef, stir-fried pork and crispy duck, and we all tuck in. I relax a little, enjoying the food.

"This is so good," I tell the others, taking a second helping of rice and chicken. "I hadn't realized how hungry I was."

"That's what you get when you work up an appetite," Marc says.

I stop with my chopsticks halfway to my mouth. Sally meets my gaze and then hastily drops hers, trying not to laugh. Hemi snorts, and his wife elbows him in the ribs. Ashton just grins.

I glare at Marc, but he's busy answering his mobile, which I can feel buzzing in his jeans where his thigh is close to mine. He takes it out and checks the screen, says, "Excuse me, I need to take this," gives me an amused look, and leaves the table, walking out of the restaurant and into the mall as he answers the call.

I look back at the others, decide humor is the best way to deal with this, and gesture at them with my chopsticks. "You can all stop smirking. He meant the visit I paid to the petting farm today."

"Yeah, yeah," Sally says. "He can't keep his eyes off you. It's quite romantic, really."

I blush and poke the chicken with the chopsticks. "I don't know about that," I mumble.

"What's the deal with Mel at the Riverbank?" Ashton asks out of the blue. "She seemed shaken to see him this afternoon, and Fitz went even more monosyllabic than he usually is when she turned up."

I hesitate—Marc obviously didn't tell him about their relationship, and I don't want to betray his confidence. Equally, we're working closely with these people, and Ashton looks genuinely perturbed.

"She's his ex," I tell him. "They broke up about five years ago."

All their eyebrows rise, and Sally exclaims, "Seriously? You mean Mel Fanshaw?"

"I don't know her surname, but he said he saw her today. Blonde bob. Pregnant."

"Holy shit," Ashton says. "No wonder both of them looked upset."

I move the noodles around the bowl, pretending to look for chicken, but in truth I've lost my appetite. I don't want to think about Marc being cut up over losing someone else. It gives me a funny feeling in the pit of my stomach.

But Sally is intrigued, and she continues, "Is Fitz the guy she was supposed to marry, the one where she canceled the wedding at the last minute?" When I nod, she presses her fingers to her lips, her eyes wide. "She told me about that. He was in an accident, wasn't he?"

"Yeah. He was in the Army," I explain, "working at Scott Base. A plane crash-landed—he wasn't on it, but it skidded across the landing strip into the yard where he was working. He fractured his pelvis and damaged several vertebrae, and had to learn to walk again."

"Jesus." Ken glances out to where Marc's pacing up and down, talking into his phone. "I'd never have guessed."

"What's she like?" I ask them, curious about the woman he was going to marry.

"A bit high-maintenance," Ashton announces. "If I'm honest."

"We get on okay," Sally says. "Lee is friends with her husband, Terry."

"Oh, I'm sorry," I say guiltily. "I didn't mean to be rude about your friend."

Lee waves a hand. "Sal knows how I feel about Mel. I've always thought she was manipulative. When I heard she'd called off a previous wedding, I was worried she'd do the same with Terry. I'm glad she didn't, although sometimes I think he'd have been better off if she had. He's a bit under the thumb."

"She is a control freak," Sally admits.

"Why did they break up?" Ashton asks her.

"She opened up about her ex one night, when a group of us had had a few drinks. She said she couldn't deal with the accident. She said she felt guilty about breaking up with him, but that the accident completely changed his personality, and he wasn't the man she'd fallen in love with."

"That's bullshit," I say, as mildly as I can, even though anger stirs inside me. "When you love someone you stand by them, in sickness and in health. She left him when he needed her most. He's still very upset about it."

"Understandably," Ashton says.

I glance out at Marc, who's studying his shoes, still on the phone. Who's he talking to? Not Mel, surely. No, it couldn't be. It's probably Noah or Leon, or maybe Izzy. Would she ring him on her honeymoon? I would imagine Hal's keeping her too busy…

As I watch, Marc sighs. I might not be great at interpreting people, but I can tell from his stance that he's upset about something. I want to go out there, slide my arms around him, and tell him I'm there for him. Again, I think what a bizarre arrangement we have, where we can be so intimate one moment—I think of what I did for him, on top of him, this afternoon, and blush—and yet in other ways not know each other at all.

I tear my gaze away and look back at the others, half wishing I hadn't told them.

But Sally smiles and says, "Don't worry, we won't say anything."

Sure enough, as Marc hangs up, slides the phone back in his pocket, and returns to the restaurant, Ashton starts up a conversation about the local elections, and by the time Marc sits, everyone's talking and laughing as we finish off the meal.

I lean a little bit closer to him and say softly, "Everything okay?"

He nods and gives a tight smile, but he pushes his plate away with the food unfinished, picks up his beer, and swallows the last few mouthfuls in one go.

I finish off my own dinner, wishing he'd confide in me. Maybe when we get back, he'll feel more relaxed and able to talk.

But after we leave the restaurant, and we're driving back to the lighthouse, despite my attempt at conversation he remains quiet, his gaze distant, and I feel our previous closeness dissipating. I want to hang onto it, but it's like mist, and I can feel it slipping through my fingers.

When we arrive and go in, I decide to give it one more shot. "Is something bothering you?" I ask. "Do you want to talk about it?"

But he shakes his head, going over instead to where we left the glasses and the bottle of whisky I brought him, and proceeds to pour us both a shot.

When Daniel was in a mood, I just turned away and busied myself with something else, but for some reason tears prick my eyes. "Is it me?" I whisper. "Have I done something to upset you?"

He looks up in surprise then, frowns, and brings the glass over. After passing it to me, he pulls me into his arms. "No, sweetheart, it's nothing to do with you."

I sniff. "Are you sure? It's not because I called you my slave?"

He laughs at that and kisses the top of my head. "Of course not. What happens in the bedroom is just play."

It's no good; I have to ask. "Was it... Mel on the phone?"

"Mel? No." He moves back to retrieve his glass. "What made you say that?"

"You said you saw her today. Ashton said it shook both of you up. I wondered whether she'd initiated communication."

"Mel would never ring me," he says, somewhat curtly, "and I have no interest in talking to her."

"Okay." I've upset him. Shit.

"Ashton knows?" he queries.

I feel ashamed that I told the crew at the Ark. "He asked me how you knew each other, so I told him. I'm sorry. I shouldn't have said anything."

He swirls the whisky around in the glass. "It's okay. It doesn't matter."

"It does, and I shouldn't have done it." I take a deep breath. "If I'm honest, I was curious as to what they thought of her."

He studies my face, but I can't tell what he's thinking. "And?" he asks.

"Ashton called her high-maintenance."

His lips curve up a little.

"I admit I felt smug when he said that," I tell him.

He gives a short laugh. "Why?" he says.

"Why what?"

"Why did you feel smug?"

"Because... she hurt my friend, and I was glad others think she isn't a nice person."

He meets my eyes. "Is that the only reason?"

Our gazes lock, and we stay like that for a long, long time. I can't answer, can't admit it, but I know he's read the truth in them.

Eventually, I look away, and he sighs and gestures to the sofa. "Let's sit down."

I sit on the sofa while he turns on the gas fire, and then he sits just down from me. He stretches out his legs and stares into the leaping flames for a while, then takes a mouthful of whisky.

"You're making me nervous," I tell him.

He turns his gaze to me. "Sorry. I'm just debating what to say. I don't talk about it much, only to Izzy, and this time I haven't even spoken to her about it."

I'm puzzled now. "Okay."

He sips his whisky. "On the phone—it was my mom. She's a recovering alcoholic, and she's currently in rehab."

Chapter Nineteen

Fitz

Poppy stares at me, bemused. "Your mother is in rehab?"

I nod, feeling the usual wave of shame and guilt. It goes against all my instincts to talk about it. But the conversation I had with Mel at the Riverbank keeps playing in my mind. Although I was angry at the time, she shocked me with the revelation that she didn't leave because of the accident, but because I wouldn't open up to her. I didn't purposefully keep things from her, but it's true that I always try to deal with things on my own. I'm not normally comfortable sharing. But it ruined that relationship. And I don't want to ruin this one, so I'm going to try to talk about it.

"She's in a special unit in Hamilton," I tell Poppy. "She's been there for a couple of weeks."

"Marc, I'm so sorry. How long has she had a problem?"

"All my life," I confess. "Although it worsened after my father died. But I can remember incidents when I was younger, too. You know about Izzy and the boiling water?"

She nods; she knows the story. When Izzy was five, my mother left a pan of hot water unattended on the stove, and Izzy tipped it over herself. It scarred her, badly enough to ensure she never wears short-sleeved tops.

"What Izzy doesn't know is that Mom wasn't in the room because she was drunk in the living room," I say.

"Oh, Jesus."

"Yeah. I can remember it happening. I was seven, and I'd just gotten home from school. She'd obviously been drinking throughout the afternoon, because I remember that when Izzy started screaming, Mom fell over trying to get to the kitchen. I've never told Izzy that."

"But she knows she drinks?" Poppy asks.

"Oh God, yeah. After our father died, Mom didn't bother hiding it any longer. She went to pieces. She left rat poison out in the garage that killed our Old English Sheepdog."

"Oh no."

"I left to go into the Army—I had to get away. I felt terribly guilty at leaving Izzy with her, though. When Izz turned eighteen, I told her she had to go to university, and persuaded her to go to veterinary college. We didn't have much money, though, and poor Izzy had to work every evening to pay her way. Several times during her first year one of us had to go home because Mom had gotten into trouble. She'd get drunk, then go out into town, cause a scene, make a nuisance of herself."

Poppy looks horrified. "How awful for you both." I'm sure the thought of the solid Charlie King or his sweet wife Ophelia doing anything like that is beyond her.

"Eventually," I continue, "it got too much. We scraped together enough money to send Mom to rehab. I had to take out a loan—again, Izzy doesn't know that. It was worth it, though; Mom made a good recovery. She ended up meeting a guy—Luke—and has lived with him ever since. She's been doing okay."

"Do you see her much? I know Izzy doesn't go down there very often."

"No, Izzy's relationship with her is complicated, and she finds it difficult to be in Mom's company. I see her a bit more often, maybe once a month. She's not an easy woman, but I try to keep an eye on her."

"So what happened recently? Why is she back in rehab?"

"I keep in touch with a woman called Rebecca, who's Mom's neighbor in Hamilton. When Mom first came out of rehab, I gave Rebecca my contact details just in case Mom had a relapse and she needed me. Rebecca has become a good friend of Mom's, and it's nice to know she has someone there if she needs them. A month or so ago, Rebecca emailed to say she thought I should know that Mom and Luke were having problems. She'd heard them arguing several times, although Mom refused to talk to her about it. I knew she'd never admit it to me, so... I'm ashamed to admit I didn't call, because I've been busy at work and, frankly, I don't need the aggravation."

"That's understandable," Poppy says, reaching out to hold my hand.

I blow out a breath. "Then, about a week later, Rebecca emailed again. Luke had walked out. Mom consoled herself with alcohol for the first time. Drunk as a skunk, she wandered into town and caused a scene outside the store where he works. He wasn't there at the time, but she broke a window, screamed and cried, then threw up outside, and someone called the police. Luke came to pick her up and took her home. I spoke to him on the phone, and he was curt and angry, and yelled that he'd had enough. I begged him to stay, at least to ensure she was all right, but a few days later he walked out again, and this time he didn't go back."

"And that tipped her over the edge."

"Yes. I haven't told Izzy about this. She was getting ready for her wedding, and I didn't want her to worry."

"That's fair enough," Poppy says, "but she won't be happy when she eventually finds out."

"I don't care." I set my jaw. "She's had a tough life, and she's finally found happiness with Hal. She deserves some time to be with him without worrying about Mom."

Poppy doesn't push it. "So you've paid for her to go back into rehab?"

"Yeah, I took her in a couple of weeks ago. Last time, she had a month-long program. This time, they've suggested she stay for two months. It'll cost twenty thousand dollars."

Poppy's eyebrows lift. "Wow."

"I've paid for the first three weeks, but..." I hesitate, but there's no point in holding back now. "I'm struggling to find the rest of the money."

Poppy's green eyes study me. I'd half expected her to say immediately that she'd give it to me, but she's cleverer than that. She knows I'd say no. "That's why you said you'd help me out," she says. "For the money."

"Partly for the money." My lips curve up. "There are a few other benefits."

She smiles, but she doesn't change the subject. "Are you going to ask Izzy to pay half?"

I look into my glass then, swirl the whisky around, and take a mouthful. "I don't want to," I reply eventually.

"She's married to one of the richest guys in New Zealand, Marc. Hal would be more than happy to help."

"I know. But I have my pride. And I don't want Izzy to know, not yet, not when she's on her honeymoon."

"Noah would give you the money."

"I know. But that's not going to happen. I'll probably get another loan." The repayments would be a problem for me, but I don't tell Poppy that. I earn a decent wage at the Ark, but I have rent and bills to pay, and I also took a loan out for my car. Noah wanted to buy it for me as a company car, but I—being an idiot—refused and bought it myself. I'll have finished paying for it in a few months, but until then, taking out another loan is going to stretch my finances to the limit.

Poppy has a mouthful of whisky and studies me, resting her cheek on the glass. "I know you're going to say no," she tells me, "but I have to say it anyway. You know I'd give you the money."

"That's very kind of you, and I appreciate it. But you know I can't take it."

She purses her lips, her brow creasing. "In that case, how about I increase your payments to two thousand dollars a night?"

"Jesus. That's not why I told you."

"I know. Come on, Marc, I know you well enough to know you'd never ask anyone for money. You're a proud man, and you're surrounded by a family for whom money has never been an issue. I can only imagine how hard that has been for you and Izzy. I've talked to her about it in the past, and she's told me how awkward she found it at veterinary college when both Hal and Stefan had money."

"I hadn't realized that," I say. "But it doesn't change anything."

"I know I'm not going to change your mind. But something you have to understand with us Kings is that it doesn't come from a position of superiority. To us, it's not a case of have and have-not. It's tough to describe what it's like growing up with money to someone who hasn't been through it. The kind of issues that most people struggle with—budgeting, waiting to get paid, saving up for holidays and birthday presents—that didn't happen with any of us. For our parents, the challenge was to give us everything we wanted without spoiling us. It's a thin line to walk, and I can't say Albie, Summer, and I didn't have issues. And of course it was even more difficult for Mom and Dad with Summer, because her birth father couldn't afford to splash out on whatever caught his eye, so they had to handle that carefully."

"I get all that, but—"

"Let me finish. I just want to say, we all have our own money through trust funds and the like, but for all of us, it's been a family thing, a shared thing. The money comes from Brock and Dad and Matt and all the hard work they did, and also from a certain amount of luck. Not every series of children's books takes off, and not every invention is a success. They're aware how lucky they are, and so are we. You think Ryan, and Summer, and Noah, don't feel guilt to some extent because they're not related to the Three Wise Men by blood?"

"I've had this conversation with Noah," I admit. "He gave me the 'we're all one big happy family' talk."

"But he's right. He created the Ark for the Kings and their friends to come together and share their lives, as well as to help animals. It was the best way he could think of to treat the money as a source that feeds all the rivers. None of us hoards our cash like Scrooge. It's there to improve everyone's lives. We all give to charity, and help where we can."

I feel a flare of irritation at being likened to a charity, but I squash it, because I know that's not what she meant. "I understand all that. But I'm not a King, and it just doesn't feel right to take that kind of money from any of you."

She nods. "That's what I thought you'd say. I'm a little disappointed, though, that you'd struggle and possibly go through hardship because of pride. I don't understand that. But life would be dull if everyone was the same."

We sip our whiskies quietly, listening to the crash of the waves on the rocks outside. The sun is setting, and the room is flooded with a dull orange light.

I can't explain how I feel to her because it's beyond my ability to vocalize my feelings. Maybe there's a tad of sexism in there—I'm a man, and deep down I feel it's my duty to look after my family. Or perhaps it's stubbornness, or shame, or a fear of having to admit I've failed. I can see she doesn't understand, and maybe she's even a little hurt that I won't accept her help. But she'll have to realize I am who I am, and I can't change overnight for her.

"Why did your mom ring tonight?" she asks. "Is she okay?"

I blow out a long breath. "It's hard to tell. She wanted to apologize to me. For making a scene again, and having the police come out. And for causing me any worry and trouble. She was sweet and sad, and it was quite hard to hear."

"I can imagine. I'm so sorry."

I shrug. I don't really want to talk about it. It was difficult to listen to Mom crying as she apologized. She knows she's been trouble for Izzy and me over the years. I've never blamed her for it, though. I suppose I could have done more to help her. Maybe I should have stayed at home and looked after her. But I don't think either of us would have wanted that. Some things are just meant to be.

"Shall we watch a movie or something?" I ask.

She nods, so I turn on the TV, and we choose a light rom-com we haven't seen. It doesn't turn out to be all that, but it raises a few laughs in us, and when it's done, we turn the lights out, lock the door, and go to bed.

I pull Poppy into my arms, her back against my chest, and nuzzle her ear. "Get some sleep," I tell her. "I'll be waking you early."

She chuckles and looks over her shoulder. "I'll hold you to that."

I kiss her lips, and then we settle down for the night. Poppy falls asleep quickly, no doubt worn out by her busy day and our enthusiastic lovemaking earlier. But thoughts whiz around in my head, refusing to die down.

I think of Izzy, off on her honeymoon with Hal, and hope she's having a good time. She's also struggled, and she was single for years. I didn't tell Poppy, but I feel partly responsible for that, because I warned Hal off her when they were teenagers, and again when he asked me to come and work at the Ark, so it's my fault they took so long to get together. I want to make it up to Izzy, and this is the only way I know how—to take the responsibility of our mother off her shoulders, and let her get on with her life.

I think of my mother, alone in her room at the rehab center, and hope she's starting to feel better. She's been in emotional pain for a lot of her life, and she deserves some happiness.

Am I dumb to refuse to ask for help? Mom is my responsibility though, and mine alone. And I can't see any other way around that.

I stare up at the stars glittering in the black velvet sky, and wait a long, long time for sleep to come.

Chapter Twenty

Poppy

I wake around five a.m. It's dark, and Marc's still asleep. I put my phone down after checking the time, wondering what woke me. I need to use the bathroom; I think that's what did it. As quietly as I can, I get up, go in and pee, then come back out and go over to the window.

There's a faint touch of color on the horizon, but the sun is almost two hours off rising, so it won't be light for a while yet. I pick up Marc's discarded T-shirt and pull it on, then tiptoe up the stairs to the viewing platform.

It's coolish up here, and I shiver a little, but it's so beautiful that I can't help but lean against the glass and look out at the view. The light above me sweeps across the ocean, illuminating the black waves briefly as it passes. When it's on the other side, I can see all the stars in the night sky.

It's so odd to be standing here, almost on the edge of the world. The Pacific is so big—it covers a third of the Earth's surface area. How thrilling it must have been to be an explorer, Magellan or Cook, setting sail without truly knowing what land was in front of you. Or to have been on one of the early Maori wakas, paddling across the ocean in search of a new home. There must have been a sense of freedom, and of excitement at a new beginning. I enjoyed traveling. I remember my OE with much fondness.

At the time, when I was staying at the monastery, I had my whole life in front of me, and I remember feeling such hope that I was on the way to finding the answer to a successful, happy life. I'm hardly old, at thirty, but it didn't quite work out the way I'd hoped. I thought I'd be married with a couple of kids and in a stable, rewarding job. I am happy in the job, but I feel some disappointment at not being settled in my personal life, to the point where I've made the decision to stay single.

Instead, here I am with a man I hardly know, trying to get pregnant. Am I mad?

"Penny for them." Marc's voice behind me makes me jump. I hadn't heard him come up the stairs. He slides his arms around my waist from behind, moves up close to me, and nuzzles my neck. He's only wearing his boxers. Mmm. I might be mad, but if I am, I don't care.

"Just thinking about the ocean," I tell him. "And how exciting it must have been to be an explorer."

"You have wanderlust in your soul, don't you?" he teases, nibbling my earlobe.

"Maybe a little."

"Do you wish you'd traveled more?"

"I don't know… perhaps." I sigh. "I was thinking about being in the monastery, and all the hopes and dreams I had when I was there."

He rests his lips on my hair. "You can't feel wistful about your achievements, surely? You've done so well. Traveled, become a teacher, and now you're in a rewarding job changing children's lives."

My lips curve up. "I like that you see it that way. But yes, I do feel a bit wistful. Everyone has dreams when they're young, don't they? About finding Mr. Right, settling down, having two-point-four kids by the time they're thirty. We all have romantic ideals about love." I place a hand over his where it rests on my ribs, under my breasts. "Do you believe in soul mates?"

"I don't know." He rests his cheek on the top of my head, looking out across the ocean. "I don't think most men have the same idealistic notions that women have when they're younger, to be honest. I don't think our expectations are as high. We don't expect perfection. We just hope we'll find someone who'll put up with our odd ways, who'll want to sleep with us from time to time, and who'll hold us at night. Or maybe I'm just getting old."

I give a short laugh. He's probably right. We all hope for that ideal person who understands us and can anticipate our every need, but nobody's perfect.

I think about Noah, who lost the love of his life, but who's now found happiness with Abby and Ethan. If we do have soul mates, does that mean he has two? Or that Abby has to take second place? Izzy and Hal, Nix and Leon, and Remy and Albie—are they all soul mates?

Or have they all settled for a person who's maybe a little more right for them than the other people they've met?

I assumed Daniel wasn't my soul mate because he made me unhappy in so many ways, but maybe I was being foolish in being dissatisfied because he wasn't perfect for me. Should I have tried harder? Attempted to make a go of the relationship? I can't bring myself to feel sorrow at our breakup, though. He was cruel to me, emotionally and, occasionally, physically—he didn't hit me or anything, but he could be quite rough. I can't imagine Marc ever saying the kind of things that Daniel said to me, and, so far anyway, he's been nothing but gentle in the bedroom. Our last session might have been a little bit more... energetic, but I can't imagine him ever hurting me.

"What are you thinking about?" he asks.

"Yesterday," I tell him. "What we did in bed."

He bends his head and kisses my neck. "Did you enjoy it?"

"Yes," I say, somewhat shyly. "I was thinking how different you are from Daniel."

"I should hope so. I don't understand any man not wanting to give their woman pleasure. It's so... satisfying." He touches his tongue to my neck, making me shiver.

"It turns you on," I whisper.

"Yes." He sucks gently, his hands rising to cup my breasts.

I tip my head back onto his shoulder and sigh. I'm hungry for him again. My body craves him like sugar; I need my fix. In fact, he's like a chocolate bar in so many ways. Being with him is a sweet treat; I want to savor each moment, make him last as long as I can.

He turns me in his arms, presses my back against the window, and lowers his mouth to mine. I part my lips for him, lift my arms, and sink my hands into his hair as he kisses me with as much passion as I'm feeling for him. Mmm... I love kissing this man. How can I have thought I didn't like kissing? There's nothing like it; it's sensual and erotic and comforting and sexy and hot all rolled into one. It's like it's a switch he flips that plugs me into the mains and turns me on— everything starts buzzing and heating up, and little ripples of pleasure run through me, connecting invisible lines between all my erogenous zones. How come when he kisses me, I feel a tug deep inside, between my legs? I want him. I want this quiet, thoughtful, wounded man to touch me, to be inside me.

Placing my hands on his chest, I push him, and he takes a step back, his eyebrows rising. I continue pushing him, and he moves backward to the sofa in the middle of the small room. I tug down his boxers, and he steps out of them, and then sinks onto the sofa as I give another little push. I lower to my knees in front of him, parting his legs, my heart beginning to race at the sight of him naked, hard and ready for me. His eyelids lower to half-mast as I lick my palm and close my hand around him, and then I stroke him, inhaling at the feel of the soft skin moving over his iron hardness. Bending, I close my mouth over the tip, and the breath hisses through his teeth, his hand rising so he can sink his fingers into my hair.

"Aaahhh…" He tips his head back, swelling in my mouth. "Poppy…"

"Mmm." He smells and tastes amazing, and I adore this power to affect him, to make him feel the way I do. He's changed me so much in such a short space of time. Before I met him, sex was a physical act for me, like sneezing or coughing, not particularly pleasurable, something I put myself through for a partner, something I endured. Now, it's physical and emotional and sensual, it's full of pleasure, and I think about it when we're not doing it; I imagine pleasing him, ways I can make him sigh.

I wish I could continue doing this until he comes, until he fills my mouth with his silky fluid, but after only a minute he holds my upper arms and lifts me, pulling me astride him.

"Aw," I complain, moving further up his thighs so our bodies are flush.

"I'm here to get you pregnant, remember? Don't want to waste any." His tone is teasing, but it reminds me why I asked him here. And for some reason, it makes me sad.

He studies my face, and I think he knows what's going through my mind, but he doesn't say anything. Instead, he cups the back of my head, brings my lips down to his, and kisses me.

His mouth is hot, insisting, and I'm already fired up from going down on him, so I can feel the blood speeding around my body, my heart racing, and I know I'm ready for him. But he makes me wait; he skims his hands down my back and around my ribs, strokes my breasts, then teases my nipples for a while, lowering his mouth to each one, and licking and sucking and tugging until I'm squirming on top of him, desperate to have him inside me.

"Stop wriggling," he scolds, dropping his hands to my hips in an attempt to keep me still.

But I push him away, lift up, and move so the tip of his erection is parting my folds. "You can't drive me crazy like this and expect me not to react."

"I drive you crazy?"

I pause with my mouth over his. "You know you do," I whisper, and then I sink down slowly, welcoming him inside me. I'm so turned on that there's no friction, and he slides in all the way up to the top.

He exhales in a soft groan, and I touch my tongue to his lip, then kiss him, drinking in his pleasure, loving every second of making love with him. I slide my hands into his hair and kiss him deeply, hungry for him, wanting to convey the feelings inside me.

I lift my head and look into his eyes, and they're full of an emotion I can't decipher. Affection? Love? No, not love. It can't be love. But there's depth of feeling there, probably because he confided in me, something I know he doesn't do with other people, and that's created an intimacy between us we can't ignore.

Keeping my gaze on his, I rock my hips, driving him in and out of me, kissing him at the same time, and we move together as if we're dancing, our bodies perfectly in sync. He lowers his mouth to my nipples and traces his tongue around them, then sucks them, and I feel an answering clench inside, and I know my climax isn't far away.

"Marc..." I tug his hair to pull his head back so I can kiss him again, and our hot mouths clash, full of yearning, of hunger. I've never felt desire like this. I never knew the heat they portray in books and the movies was real. Ooh, that feels good, I'm so close, so close...

And then he holds me tightly around the waist and moves, and I'm falling backward, onto the carpet. I squeal, but he's holding me, and he lowers me onto my back, still inside me.

"My turn to be in charge," he says, and then he starts moving, really thrusting, driving inside me in a way he hasn't done before. And oh God, that's hot; my body is so aroused, and I'm so ready for him that it sends me tumbling toward the edge. He's propped on his hands and I can tell he's lost it, that his body is taking over, and he wants me, oh God he wants me, and I come, pulsing again and again, clenching around him as I cry out in ecstasy.

He rides me through it, his muscles tight, his body taut, and then he comes too. I hold him, knowing he's spilling inside me, and I cry because it's so beautiful and I love it so much, and I don't ever want him to stop.

When he's done, he kisses my face, my eyes, kisses away my tears.

"We've made a baby tonight," he says, not questioning that I'm upset, kissing back to my mouth.

"You sound so certain," I whisper, sniffing.

"I am. I know it, one hundred percent."

It's sentimental, because of course he can't know, but I kinda hope he's right. I want his baby. I want a little piece of him I can hang onto when he's gone.

A piece of him I can love forever.

Chapter Twenty-One

Fitz

It's late afternoon, a few days later, and we're at the new Ark, working. The wind blows across the fields, bringing with it the smell of the sea, and all of a sudden I feel homesick.

It's odd, because I wasn't born in the Bay of Islands, and I haven't spent that many years there, in terms of a percentage of my life. But it's only now I realize how I've felt at home since moving there five years ago. I think maybe a small part of my soul had lingered in Hawke's Bay, as if it had snagged on barbed wire, leaving behind little tufts of memory that meant I wasn't completely whole. But now I'm back here, I feel as if I've finally pulled free. Seeing Mel was hard, but it has liberated me, too. She doesn't have a claim on me anymore. She has her own family, and it's time for me to move on.

I'm not quite sure what moving on is going to involve for me yet. But I have an idea.

I stand by the fence, half-listening to Ashton as he talks about where he's thinking of placing the car park, my gaze drifting across to Poppy. She's sitting in the plastic chairs with Sally and Hemi over by the office block, drinking coffee, shading her eyes from the bright sun. Her beautiful hair is loose, and it looks like fire in the sunlight. She's so beautiful. And she's completely captured my heart.

I half expected it to happen while we were away, and yet it feels so different from what I anticipated. I knew I'd enjoy sleeping with her, and I thought we'd fit together, that it would feel comfortable, because we have so much in common. We're so similar—for example, we don't feel the need to fill every gap in the conversation; we enjoy just being in each other's company. One of my favorite things is lying in bed after we've made love, her lying half across me, tracing my fingers up and down her back, with our thoughts drifting. Mel always wanted to know what I was thinking and feeling, but Poppy's not like that. She's so easy to be with.

It's been an idyllic few days. We've worked hard, spending a lot of hours with Ashton and the others, sharing knowledge that's been really useful. We've also been out and about, including a trip to Hastings' twin city, Napier, up the coast a little. The city was razed in an earthquake in 1931—still New Zealand's deadliest natural disaster with 256 people killed—and much of the destroyed town center was rebuilt in the Art Deco tradition. Poppy loved the bold geometric forms, the sunbursts and fountains, and the skyscraper shapes, and she bought several pieces of art to take back home.

We've also had an amazing few days in the bedroom. I finally got to use the spray cream, and licked it off every place I could think, driving her crazy. We've made love so many times we're both exhausted, and my hip twinges occasionally from all the exercise. If she's not pregnant, it's not for the want of trying. But it's coming to the end of the week now. Part of me wants to stay here forever, in that lighthouse with her. But I long for the bay, and I also know it's time for us to decide where we go from here.

"Penny for them," Ashton says. "As if I have to ask."

I shift my gaze to him and give him a wry look. "Sorry."

"No worries. Your view is much more attractive than mine." He smiles. "You going to carry on seeing her when you get back to the bay?"

I hesitate, glancing back at her. "Not sure yet. Hopefully."

"She told Sally she's recovering from a bad relationship."

"Yeah."

"Afraid of getting hurt again?" Ashton suggests.

"Definitely."

"Am I making you feel awkward?"

I laugh and kick the bottom of the fence. "Nah."

"Man of few words," Ashton says, and grins.

I turn and lean back on the fence, sliding my hands into the pockets of my jeans. Although Poppy and I don't talk all the time, I find it easy to confide my thoughts to her. I've opened up to her more in one week than I ever did with Mel. And I've been surprised how that's made me feel. Sometimes it's nice to share your troubles with someone.

"We've both had tricky relationships," I admit. The words don't come easy, as if my mouth is rusty. "And she's not keen on settling down with anyone. But I'm hoping I can change her mind."

"Well, she's crazy about you," Ashton comments. "That's obvious."

My gaze lingers on her again. Is he right? When I asked her, *I drive you crazy?* She replied, *You know you do.* I know I've changed her. She was so convinced a woman couldn't come during sex, and we've proven how wrong that theory was over and over again. Now she's more confident in bed, expecting to have the same kind of pleasure as the guy, and knowing how to take it. I'm glad I've done that for her. But is it enough to convince her I'm right for her?

And suddenly, I know what I want to say.

"Take five?" I suggest to Ashton. He nods, turning back to his plan for the car park, and I wander across the drive to the three of them sitting in the chairs. "Got a minute?" I ask Poppy.

Her eyebrows rise, and then she nods and gets up from the chair. I lead her away from the others, around the corner of the office block, so we have a little privacy, and we walk slowly along the path, looking out across the fields.

Poppy doesn't ask me what's up or demand to know why I've whisked her away; she lifts her face to the sun and inhales the fresh spring air, just enjoying being there. I'm so in love with this girl.

"So we're off tomorrow," I say.

She opens her eyes and looks up at me. "Yes. I'm both disappointed and looking forward to going home."

"Me too. I hope you've had a good time here."

She smiles. "Of course. It's been amazing."

I can't help it—I pull her toward me, cup her face, and lower my lips to hers. She tastes sweet, of summer, which is just around the corner, and her hair is soft, curling around my fingers. I tilt my head to the side, slanting my lips across hers, and she opens her mouth eagerly, her tongue sliding against mine. Ohhh… she fires me up in just a few seconds, and I'm tempted to grab her hand, drag her to the car, drive her back to the lighthouse, and make love to her again, even though we only did it a few hours ago.

But I move back and lower my hands, determined to see this through. "I want to talk to you about what happens when we get back," I say.

She sucks her bottom lip, and immediately her eyes become wary.

"Don't look like that," I tell her softly.

"I know what you're going to say," she whispers. "I did tell you I wasn't interested in a relationship."

"I know."

"I said I wouldn't let myself fall for you."

I swallow hard. "I know. But doesn't how I feel come into it?"

She looks away, across the fields, where the spring flowers are waving in the breeze. "Marc…"

"I love you." There. I've said it.

Her gaze snaps back to mine, and her eyebrows rise. "What?"

"I love you," I repeat, with more conviction.

"You can't," she states. "We've been together one week."

"I don't recall seeing an instruction manual. Is there a set amount of time you have to have dated, then?"

"We're not dating."

"No, we're just having sex. There's no emotion there at all."

Her expression softens. "Of course there's emotion."

I move closer to her and brush my lips to hers. "Are you really telling me you don't have any feelings for me at all?"

She reaches up into the kiss, I move back a fraction, and she lowers back down, a tad resentful. "No, I'm not saying that."

"What if you are pregnant? Have you thought about it? About how we're going to deal with it?" I can see immediately from her face that she hasn't. She might have thought about having a baby, but she's carefully blanked out any thought of the father from her mind.

"I hope you are pregnant," I tell her. "But that's not what this is about. I want to be with you. And that's why I want to ask you…" I take a deep breath. "Poppy, will you—"

My phone rings.

My mouth stumbles on the words. "Dammit." I yank the phone out, about to cancel the call. Then I frown as I see the number of the rehab unit where my mother's staying. I blow out a long breath.

Poppy glances at the phone in my hand. "You should take that."

"I can call back."

"Take it," she says. "Then we'll finish the conversation."

I meet her gaze for a moment. She knows what I was about to say. She's going to take the time to formulate a reply. I curse the phone, but I do need to answer, so without another word I turn and walk away and put the phone to my ear.

"Yes?" I snap.

"Marc?"

I force myself to concentrate. "Yes."

"It's Wendy Orpington, the manager of the Crossroads Rehabilitation Unit."

"Hello, Wendy."

"Good morning. Marc, where are you?"

It's a strange question, and I frown. "In Hawke's Bay."

"Are you sitting down?"

"What? No. Why?"

"I have something to tell you, and I'd prefer it if you were sitting down."

There's nowhere to sit, and now I'm worried. Has Mom had another relapse? "What is it?"

"Marc, I'm so sorry, but I'm afraid I have to tell you that your mother died last night."

I stare across the fields, although I'm not seeing anything. "What?"

"I'm very sorry. She suffered a heart attack during the night."

I go completely cold, and for a moment I think I'm going to faint. "Jesus."

Poppy appears beside me, her hand on my back. "Marc? What is it?"

I can't think straight and just look at her blankly. "What happened?" I ask Wendy.

"We went into her room this morning when she didn't show for breakfast. She'd passed away a few hours before, in her sleep, from what we can tell. She'd shown no signs of heart disease, and she was doing well in her recovery. She didn't suffer, we don't think. We will hold an enquiry, but I'm afraid it was just one of those things. I am so very sorry."

I can't make sense of the words. Mom's dead? My heart races, and my head spins.

Turning, I bend and vomit suddenly onto the flowerbed. It comes out of nowhere, and I'm powerless to stop it.

Poppy gently takes the phone from my hand, and I half hear her talking in the background as I struggle to regain my composure, my hands on my knees.

"Hello?" Poppy says. "I'm Marc's friend, Poppy King. May I ask what's happened? Oh Jesus, I see. When? Right. Oh, how awful. Yes, of course, I understand. No, I'm sure you did everything you could. He's okay, just in shock. Look, I'm going to give you my mobile number, can you ring me if you need anything? Yes, Hawke's Bay. I'll get us on the next plane to Hamilton. Can you give me the address?"

She continues talking, and I feel a flood of thankfulness that she's with me, taking over, because at this moment I don't think I can put two words together. I take deep, shaky breaths. Get a grip, Fitz. Pull yourself together. But it's impossible. I can't believe it. My mother died. She was alone, without her family, without her partner. I think she loved Luke, but she never got over the death of my father, and she never really recovered from her alcoholism. It's plagued her all her life. What a vicious disease. And now she's gone. I hope she wasn't in too much pain. Oh God, I can't bear to think about it. Both my parents are gone now. I'm completely alone, except for Izzy. Oh Jesus, Izzy. I'm going to have to ring her on her honeymoon. My heart aches at the thought of having to tell her. She'll want to come home. They're due back in two days anyway, so she might as well hang on. She's going to take it hard.

My thoughts are jumbled, like a kite in the sky, being tossed by the wind. I straighten as Poppy hangs up the call, and she comes over to me.

"Honey, I'm so sorry," she says, touching my face.

I wipe my mouth, conscious of having vomited. "Sorry about that."

"It's shock. It's okay. Come on, we need to get you sitting down."

"I should have finished the call; did you apologize to Wendy for me?"

"She's fine, she understands. Everything will be okay."

"It won't." My throat tightens. "Mom's gone."

Poppy's eyes glimmer with tears. "I know."

"I can't believe it. She died."

"Wendy said it was in her sleep. She didn't even know about it."

Is that a consolation? Just drifting away one night, not even being aware you're going?

"What I mean is, at least she wasn't in pain," Poppy corrects.

I nod. "She'd been in pain for so much of her life. I should have been there. At the end. Nobody should die alone."

"We all die alone," Poppy says. "It's those who share their lives with someone who are the lucky ones."

I meet her eyes. I'd been about to propose to her, but I can't do it now. I can't think of anything except the gaping hole that's suddenly opened up in my life.

"Come on," she whispers. "Let's get back to the lighthouse and pack, and I'll call for the plane to pick us up and take us to Hamilton."

Chapter Twenty-Two

Poppy

After telling Ashton and the others, who are all as shocked at the suddenness of the announcement as Marc and I are, we say our goodbyes, and I drive us back to the lighthouse. I've already rung the pilot of our plane to come and collect us, and we have about two hours before we're due to take off.

Marc is silent beside me, looking out of the window, white-faced. I can't imagine what he's going through. He'd already lost his father, and now his mother; he's an orphan at thirty-two. It shouldn't happen that way. Your parents should live into their seventies or eighties, and get to play with their grandchildren. This is all wrong.

We arrive at the lighthouse, and I ask him whether he wants to stay in the car while I pack, but he shakes his head and comes inside with me. We move around quietly, packing up our stuff. I don't speak, and neither does he.

He goes upstairs while I finish putting the groceries into a box, and I hear him unzipping his case and putting away his clothes. I stop for a minute and look out of the window, tears pricking my eyes. Not for Jocelyn, not really, as I'd never met her, but for him and Izzy, and also for myself, that the week had to end like this.

At the Ark, he told me he loves me, that he wants to be with me, and then he said, *And that's why I want to ask you… Poppy, will you—*

Maybe he was just going to ask me to continue seeing him. But something tells me he was going to propose.

Holy moly.

What would I have said if he had? I think I knew deep down that this was a risk if I agreed to us sleeping together. Not a risk that he'd propose, but that he'd want to continue with a relationship. Of course

I did. I like him, a lot, and even though I turned him down back in July, the thought of sleeping with him was too tempting to refuse.

But now this has happened, complicating things a hundredfold. He's not going to be in any state of mind to think about his future for a while. And that's fair enough. All I can do is be there for him and try to help.

My eyes sting as I think of how shocked he was when he heard. It must have been so hard for him and Izzy over the years to deal with Jocelyn without giving up their own lives and dreams to look after her. Oh God, Izzy. Marc's going to have to ring her in Fiji. That's going to be a difficult call.

I jerk myself out of my musings and finish off packing, then go up the stairs to the bedroom. He's not in there, although all his stuff's packed. I finish putting my clothes in my case quickly, and throw in the bathroom bag, take a final glance around, then go up the stairs to the viewing platform.

He's standing by the window, his hands in the pockets of his jeans. I can tell from his breathing that he's struggling not to cry, although I can see his face is wet. He lifts a hand and brushes over it, and gives a shaky sigh. I don't know whether he would rather I leave him for a while, but it's not in my nature to do that. I know I can't make him feel better, but I want to bring him comfort.

So I walk up behind him, slide my arms around his waist, and hug him.

He puts a hand over mine and leans his forehead on the window. "I can't believe she's gone."

Tears run down my face and I tighten my arms. "I know. I'm so sorry."

"Can you… give me five minutes…"

I kiss between his shoulder blades. "Of course."

"I'm sorry. It's just…"

"Don't worry about it. Come down when you're ready."

I release him and go out, closing the door behind me.

I take the bags out to the car and pack it up, then sit outside on the step in the sunshine. He doesn't want to lose control in front of me. I shouldn't be surprised. He's such a private person. So self-contained and solitary. I bet he misses Jack right now. A man needs his dog at times like this.

I take out my phone and study it. Everyone at the Ark will want to know. I'll call Noah in a minute—he'll pass the message on to everyone. First, though, I dial my father's number in and call him.

He answers within a few rings. "Charlie King."

"Dad?" I swallow hard as, immediately, my eyes fill with tears. "It's me."

"Poppy? Hello, sweetheart. How's it going in Hawke's Bay?"

I'd rung to tell him I was going down there to check out the new Ark. He knew I was going with Marc, but he didn't query it. I'm not sure whether he was being tactful or clueless. Either is a possibility.

"It's fine," I say. "Or it was. We've just heard that Marc's mom has died."

"Oh no. Jocelyn, isn't it?"

"Yes."

"How?"

I tell him about the heart attack, and what Wendy told me. "She passed away in her sleep, apparently."

"You'd be surprised how often that happens." As always, Dad's a doctor first. It gives him a practicality I've always loved. "It's good that she wasn't in pain, anyway."

"That's what I said, but it's come as such a shock to Marc. I mean, she was in rehab for her alcoholism, but obviously he never expected this."

"How is he?"

"As you'd expect. We've literally only just heard. He asked me to leave him alone for a few minutes." I want to explain why that makes me sad, but I can't.

"Some people grieve best with others," Dad says. "Some grieve best alone, especially men. It doesn't mean anything. I'm sure he's very glad to have you there."

"I don't know," I squeak. "I think I might have screwed things up a bit."

"Aw, I doubt it. We Kings tend to think we're disastrous at love, but it usually works out."

I wipe my eyes. He knows we're here together. I should have guessed.

"You want me to call Noah?" Dad asks. "Tell him about Jocelyn?"

"Oh, would you? He'll tell everyone else. But can you make sure they don't call Hal and Izzy? Marc will want to do that."

"Yes, of course. Are you coming home now?"

"No, I'll go with Marc to Hamilton, for a bit at least. I'm not sure what he's going to want to do, or if he'll want my help." I'm floundering; I'm not Marc's wife, and I'm not even his girlfriend. I have no social standing. He's not going to want to try to explain our relationship to everyone while he's grieving. But then again I am his friend, aren't I? I'd help if it was anyone else at the Ark.

"Look," Dad says, "*kia kaha*, sweetheart. Stay strong. Marc will need you now, whether he knows it or not. Be there for him, and when it's all done, you'll be able to talk about where you go from here. Okay?"

"Okay."

"You know where I am if you need anything. And expect a call from Noah; he's bound to ring once he hears."

"Yeah, okay. Thanks, Dad."

"See you soon." He hangs up.

I wipe my face and get to my feet as I hear Marc's footsteps on the stairs. He comes outside and stops before me. "Sorry about that," he murmurs. His eyes are red, but he looks composed.

"It's okay. I just spoke to Dad, and he's going to ring Noah. I asked Noah to make sure nobody calls Izzy and Hal, though. I thought you'd want to do that. Unless you want Noah to, or me?"

"No, I'll do it now, I think. We have a bit of time before we have to go to the airport, don't we?"

"Yes. Would you like a glass of whisky?"

"Oh man, I'd love one."

I rub his arm. "I'll pour you one while you make the call."

I leave him to it, watching out of the window as I retrieve the bottle of whisky from the box and pour some into a glass. He dials and walks away, toward where the sea breaks on the rocks, sending a couple of seagulls into the air. He starts talking, so I know Izzy has answered, and I watch as he pinches the bridge of his nose with two fingers, then runs his hand through his hair and tips his face up to the sun. I cover my mouth with a hand, full of emotion, wishing I could make it better for them. Poor Izzy, on her honeymoon and receiving such terrible news. I know she didn't get on with her mother, and didn't see her very often. But that's not going to make it any easier. It might even make it harder, because she's bound to feel guilt at not seeing her more.

I wait for him to finish the call, then go out and hand him the glass. He drinks half of it in one go, and we both look out over the ocean, to where the sky is slowly darkening, turning the sea orange.

"It's a stupid question," I say, "but how is she?"

"Shocked. Angry."

"At you?"

"No, at Mom. For dying without us." He gives me a crooked smile. "I spoke to Hal briefly. He's going to try to convince her to stay another night until their flight's due. There's no point her rushing back. We can wait and have the funeral in a couple of weeks."

"Will you have it in Hamilton?"

"I don't know. To be honest, she didn't have any friends, apart from Rebecca, her neighbor."

"What about her partner, Luke, wasn't it? Do you think he'll want to go?"

"I don't know," Marc says. "I suppose I should ring him and tell him—I doubt he knows."

"Do you have his number?"

"Yes, it's on my phone. I'd better do that now."

"I'll get you a refill," I tell him, take his glass, and go back inside. By the time I've poured the next glass, he's finished the call.

"Short and sweet," he says when I go back out, taking the glass from me. "He didn't say much. He wants to go to the funeral."

"He'll be feeling guilty, no doubt," I say.

Marc shrugs. "It wasn't his fault. I don't blame him for leaving. She could be difficult." He stops and scuffs at a stone with his shoe. "I shouldn't say that. Not now."

I rub his arm. "It's all right. There's only me here. She had a hard life, and she struggled a lot with her issues. But she knew you were always there for her. She must have been so proud of you and Izzy, with all that you've achieved."

His gaze caresses my face, and then he pulls me into an embrace with his free hand, and kisses my forehead. "How do you always know the right thing to say?"

"It's very rare. Usually I'm the first to screw things up."

He gives a short laugh. I slide my arms around his waist, and we stand there like that for a while, as he sips his whisky, the seagulls crying around us.

"You said 'It's those who share their lives with someone who are the lucky ones,'" he comments. "You know I'm going to want to talk to you about that later, don't you?"

"Yes." I bury my nose in his T-shirt, trying not to cry. I feel such a sense of hope mixed in with the sorrow. He still wants me. There's so much promise here, as if we've planted seeds in the spring and are waiting for signs of growth. But those new shoots are vulnerable to the elements. Can I bear to hang around and see if they take?

"I want to wait, though," he says. "Get this out of the way, get the funeral done. So I can think clearly."

"That makes sense."

"You'll think about it, too? I know what you told me originally, that you wouldn't let yourself fall for me, but I hope you really think about us, and what we've had this week. I think we could have something really good, and I hope you agree."

I nuzzle his neck, breathing in his scent. "I know we could."

"Loving isn't easy," he says. "Loving people is hard. It means being open and vulnerable, and letting yourself be in a position to be hurt. It doesn't matter if that person is a lover or a friend or a relative."

"I know."

"Just… think about that. Because the question is coming, and I'm going to want an answer."

"I know."

He finishes off his whisky. "All right. Come on then, let's get to the airport and get it all done."

Chapter Twenty-Three

Poppy

The next ten days pass agonizingly slowly for me. I try to be there for Marc as much as I can, but after Izzy gets home on Sunday, the two of them decide to take a week off and fly back to Hamilton to make the final arrangements for the funeral, and to go to Jocelyn's house and sort through all her stuff.

I'd like to have gone with him, but I sense it's a time for brother and sister to reconnect and grieve together, and Hal's staying at the Ark, so I don't feel as if I can offer to go with Marc.

He does call me every night, when he gets back to the hotel—neither he nor Izzy wanted to stay at Jocelyn's house. We talk for a while, and he tells me about the state of the house—that it's full of junk they're having to sort through, and I tell him what's been going on at the Ark. I'd love to chat for longer, but he sounds exhausted, so I don't keep him for long. He finishes by softly telling me he loves me, and I tell him I love him too, because it feels awkward not to say it back.

Do I mean it? I ponder on it after I hang up. I'm not sure. I miss him beside me at night, curled around me, his chest to my back, his arms holding me tightly. His hand stroking my back in the early morning, before dipping lower, waking me up in the best way possible. I miss sitting on the two-seater sofa in the living room of the lighthouse, watching TV while we sip our whisky, or looking out at the stars up in the viewing room, in the darkness. I miss his kisses, the way he taught me so tenderly to accept him, and to explore my own pleasure. I miss his low chuckle, his wry sense of humor, his quiet, solid manner. I miss him.

But there's no time to talk about it, and so I know I'm just going to have to wait until he gets back, when we can talk about it further.

He and Izzy return for a couple of days, during which he's super busy at the Ark. He doesn't ask me to stay at his place, and so I don't mention it either. We catch up at work a couple of times, but he's brisk and businesslike, and I don't push it.

It's Noah who tells me that Marc and Izzy have decided to have a private cremation for Jocelyn in Hamilton, to give Jocelyn's neighbor and Luke a chance to say goodbye, and then they're going to have the wake in the bay, at Noah's house, at his suggestion. He tells me that, this time, Hal's flying down with her for the funeral. Marc doesn't ask me to go, though, and I don't offer because I'm not sure I can face the rejection.

I've hardly spoken to him over the past few days, and I feel forlorn and adrift. I also feel achy, as if I'm coming down with something. It could be PMS. Or it could be something else.

The day before the funeral, I check my calendar for the umpteenth time and confirm—it's day twenty-nine of my cycle. My period usually starts around day twenty-nine, sometimes twenty-eight, and the test I've bought says it can tell if you're pregnant from when you're one day late, so I know it's time to try it.

When I get home from work, having thought about it all day, I go into the bathroom and, with shaking hands, I pee on the stick. While I wash my hands, my heart races. I feel excited and panicky and a little sad, all rolled into one. I'd kinda hoped I might be doing this with Marc by my side, but that obviously wasn't to be. Wasn't this what I wanted? To do it alone? I told him I didn't want a relationship—that I wouldn't let myself fall for him. I look at my reflection in the bathroom mirror and see tears glistening in my eyes. I've been five kinds of idiot, as usual, useless at dealing with people, with no idea of how to handle a relationship. Fancy agreeing to sleep with a guy just to get pregnant. I'm such a fool. I was always going to fall in love with him, wasn't I?

I turn over the stick.

There's no line in the large square. I'm not pregnant.

I stare at it. I'm not pregnant?

We've made a baby tonight, Marc told me that night he tipped me onto the carpet in the viewing room. *I know it, one hundred percent.* Unfortunately, he was wrong.

I sit on the toilet seat, my legs suddenly shaky. I keep staring at the test, just in case I haven't left it long enough, and the line's going to suddenly appear. But it doesn't. I'm definitely not pregnant.

I blow out a long breath. It's good news. It was a stupid arrangement anyway. It would have been really awkward knowing the father, and I know he would have made a fuss, and wanted to be involved. This way, I can go back to my original idea and do it the way I wanted. Cold and clinical. With no emotion involved at all.

I put my hand over my mouth and burst into tears.

*

The next day is the day of the funeral. In the morning, Leon flies Marc, Izzy, and Hal down to Hamilton in the helicopter for the cremation. The Ark stays open until two p.m., with Stefan, Clio, and Summer manning the veterinary center, and then we close, go home and get dressed, and come back to Noah's house by four p.m., ready for the wake.

By the time I arrive, Brock and Erin are there, and Matt and Georgia, and Dad turns up just after me. Mom is in Australia at the moment, visiting my grandmother—her own mother, who hasn't been well lately. Half of me wishes I'd gone with her. I miss her, and it would be nice to see my grandmother. Everyone from the Ark is there, along with lots of dogs, and the caterers that Noah has hired are just starting to hand out glasses of champagne when someone shouts that the helicopter has arrived.

Some people go outside to welcome them back, but I stay inside, helping Abby put the finishing touches to the fruitcake she's made.

"You okay?" she murmurs once we're on our own. "You've been very quiet since you got back."

"I'm fine." I give her a quick smile. The truth is that I feel awful. I'm nervous about seeing Marc again, and I'm not looking forward to the conversation we might or might not be having.

"You're not…" She leaves the question open, and I remember telling her before we left to go to Hawke's Bay that Marc was hoping to get me pregnant.

"No," I admit, trying to ignore the hollow feeling I have deep inside. "Unfortunately not."

"Oh well," Abby says brightly, "next time for sure, eh?"

I just smile, not wanting to go into it all. She studies my face and opens her mouth to respond, but at that moment Izzy and Marc come through the door, and so the moment passes.

Izzy looks pale, and her eyes are red-rimmed, but she laughs as Noah says something and presses a glass of champagne into her hand,

and accepts a kiss on the cheek from him. Everyone goes up to them to give their condolences.

I sip my champagne, unable to tear my eyes away from Marc. He's wearing a dark-gray suit, a white shirt, and a black tie, and he looks so handsome it makes my heart ache. God, I've missed him so much. I wait for him to see me and come over. Will he hug me or kiss me in front of everyone? At that moment, I wouldn't have cared if he had. I want him to. I just want to touch him, to hold him.

He straightens from giving someone a hug and his gaze scans the room. It falls on me, and he pauses for a second. I can hardly breathe, and my heart is banging against my ribs.

He gives a small smile. Then someone says something behind him, and he turns away to talk to them.

That's it. That's all I get. That's all I'm worth. I'm not a wife, not a girlfriend. Just a girl he banged for a week while he was on holiday.

It's unfair, and I know it, but my eyes fill with tears. And suddenly, I know I can't stay.

As quietly and unobtrusively as I can, I pick up my purse and slip out of the open door.

I run down the path to the main car park. Nobody tries to stop me. It's a beautiful spring afternoon, and the Pacific is a stunning blue, but I can't see its beauty today. I get in my car, start it up, and leave the Ark behind me.

I drive through Paihia, the sea on my left, tears pouring down my face. I've been such a fool. I've lost everything. Marc, the relationship, and the dream of having a baby with him.

Why didn't I tell him at the time that I loved him? That what I wanted deep down was to have a family with him? Why did I insist on staying aloof? It's all my own fault, and that hurts more than Daniel's cruelty ever did.

I reach my house without even remembering the drive there, park, and go inside. It's cool and quiet, filled with sunshine. I stand in the middle of the room and let the tears pour down my face. Oh God, this was what I *didn't* want. I didn't want to fall in love because when it all goes wrong, it hurts so much. I told myself I wouldn't let this happen! Why didn't I follow my own instructions?

I manage to make it to the sofa, sink down, and curl up on my side. I keep thinking about that smile he gave me. Full of pity and regret. Just the memory makes me ache.

God, I'm such a fool.

*

There's a knock at the door.

I unfurl and look at my phone. It's only been twenty minutes. I know I must look a sight. I've been ugly crying, and my hands are streaked with black, so I know my makeup has run. I'm so stuffed up I can't breathe. I don't want to see anyone.

The knock is insistent, though, and then, to my surprise, I hear my father's voice. "Poppy! I know you're in there. Let me in, please, sweetheart."

"Dad?" I get up, go over to the door, and open it.

"Wow," he says, his eyebrows rising. "Mascara explosion."

I burst into tears again. "Don't make fun of me," I sob.

"Aw, honey. This isn't like you. Come here." He walks into the house, closes the door behind him, and takes me in his arms.

He smells comforting and familiar, bringing back memories of sitting on his lap as a girl while we watched TV. "It's all right," he soothes, leading me over to the sofa. "Everything's going to be all right."

"It's not." We sit, and I cry into his shirt, conscious I'm covering it in black blotches and not caring.

"You've got to give him time." He kisses the top of my head. "He's just lost his mother. Guys take that hard sometimes."

"It's not that." I try desperately to wipe my face and fail. He takes his silk pocket square out and hands it to me. I stare at it doubtfully, and he flaps it in the air, so I take it and blow my nose, then try to clear my tears. "I thought I was pregnant, and I'm not." It's no good—fresh tears appear as soon as I wipe the others away.

"Oh," Dad says. "Right. So... you wanted to get pregnant?"

I nod miserably. "I asked Marc to be a sperm donor, and he said he'd only help me get pregnant if we did it the old-fashioned way."

Dad gives a short laugh, then purses his lips as I look at him. "Sorry. But I have to admire his approach. That was pretty ballsy."

"I wanted a baby," I whisper, and give a little hiccup. "Someone of my own to love, who wouldn't leave me."

Dad sighs and leans back, taking me with him. "Even children leave you eventually," he advises. "They go out into the world and become amazing teachers, and break your heart."

"Aw, Dad. Are you trying to make me cry even more?"

He rubs my back. "So you were trying to get pregnant while you were away?"

I nod. "But I took a test yesterday, and I'm not."

"Well, it's not the end of the world. Maybe you just need more practice." He smiles.

"No, I think we're done," I tell him. "I said to Marc that I didn't want a relationship, and that I wouldn't let myself fall for him. He doesn't think I'm interested."

"So tell him you are."

"Dad, it's not that easy."

"It really is. What do you have to lose?"

I glower at him. "My pride. My dignity."

"I lost those a long time ago. They're not really worth anything, believe me, when love is in the offing."

Love? Yes, I love Marc. I know I do. Oh, I'm such an idiot.

I shift on the sofa, lowering a hand over my tummy. "I wish I didn't ache so much."

"Period pain?"

"No. I'm waiting for it to start. I think I caught a cold in Hawke's Bay."

Dad raises an eyebrow at me. I shake my head. "I told you, I took a test yesterday. It was negative."

"How late are you?" he asks.

"Two days. But I feel achy—I know it's going to start any minute."

"Sore boobs?"

"Um, well, yeah."

"Overly emotional? Feeling queasy?"

I just stare at him. Come to think of it...

"So you took a test when you were a day late?" he says.

"Yes. Although sometimes my cycle is twenty-nine days. But the test says it's accurate most of the time..."

He sighs. "Sweetheart, if you ovulated one day later than normal, the test might not have picked it up yet."

My heart is beginning to race. "No, that's not possible..."

"Trust me, I'm a doctor. Do you have another test here?"

"Yes, but—"

He lifts his arm. "Go and take it."

I stare at him. "Seriously?"

"Humor me."

I get up in a huff. "Okay, but when I'm right, you're going to owe me another test. They're not cheap."

He pretends to check his pockets. "I think I have a billion dollars in here somewhere…"

Pulling a face, I go off to the bathroom. I know he's wrong; I know I did the test right before. But my heart still races as I take off the package and pee on the stick. I wash my hands, then look up at my reflection. Dear God, I look like an extra from *The Rocky Horror Show*. I scrub under my eyes, trying to shift the black, but it's waterproof mascara and I need to cleanse it properly. I sigh and toss the tissue in the bin, knocking the test off the sink in the process. Mumbling under my breath, I bend and pick it up.

And stare at it.

The large square has a line in it.

I'm pregnant.

Dad taps on the door. "Poppy?"

I open it and look up at him, eyes streaming.

"Told you," he says, leaning against the doorjamb with his hands in his pockets.

"Oh my God." I cover my mouth with my hand. "I'm pregnant."

"I'm going to be a grandad again," he says. "Oh man, I'm getting old."

I make a sound like a squeak, and he laughs and puts his arms around me. "My own baby is having a baby," he whispers. "There's something extra special about that."

The words mean a lot to me. I know he loves Summer, and he's worked extra hard all his life to try to develop a cure for her CF, and to make her feel as if she's a part of his family as much as his own children. Because of this, there have been times I've been jealous of her. She has two fathers to love her, for a start. She's older than me, more confident, and she doesn't have the social difficulties I have. She fell for Zach at a young age and the two of them have been deliriously happy. Dad calls her boys his grandkids, and I've never begrudged her that. But for him to acknowledge, just between the two of us, that this is special touches me to the core.

"I'm such a mess," I whisper.

"I know. Me too. And your brother. It's amazing how we find people to put up with us."

"What am I going to do about Marc?"

"What do you want to do?"

"I don't know."

"Well maybe you should give it some thought before you talk to him."

I've got to tell him I'm pregnant. I feel dizzy at the thought.

Just then, there's a knock at the door.

"Poppy?" Marc yells. "It's me."

"Oh my God." I pull back from Dad and look at my face in the mirror. "I can't see him now. Look at the state of me."

"Wash your face," he instructs. "I'll keep him occupied."

"How?"

"I don't know. I'll sing a song." He kisses my cheek. "Love you."

I watch him go, feeling a swell of happiness and excitement in my heart, swiftly followed by a surge of nerves. I have no idea how this is going to go.

I rest my hand over my belly. I'm pregnant. With Marc's child. Holy shit.

Nothing's ever going to be the same again. So why pretend it is?

Chapter Twenty-Four

Fitz

The door opens to reveal Charlie King, with his usual affable smile and gray ruffled hair. I knew he was here because I saw his car outside. He'd obviously seen Poppy leave the party and wanted to make sure she was all right, too.

I've met Charlie a few times at the Ark. He's like his daughter in a lot of ways—quiet, thoughtful, a lot going on behind his eyes. I'm sure he would have been very like Albie at his age; maybe a little less carefree, a little more serious. He's obviously highly intelligent, which is intimidating, but he's so nice with it that it doesn't matter.

"Hey Fitz," he says, standing back. "And hey Jack." He ruffles the dog's hair where I hold him under my arm. "Come in."

I walk into Poppy's house for the first time, put Jack down, and glance around. It's not at all what I thought. Her office is sparse and businesslike, all chrome and glass, and I'd expected her home to be the same. It's not. Pieces of stylish wooden furniture stand dotted about, and the place is filled with color—paintings, throws, and cushions, all adding splashes of bright yellows, reds, blues, and greens. She must have picked up a lot of them on her travels, I think, or at least they have an Indian theme to them.

She's not here, and I give Charlie a quizzical look. "Composing herself," he says. "I told her I'd entertain you with a song, but you really don't want to hear me sing. Want a Coke instead?"

I like that he hasn't asked me why I'm here, or why I've left the wake Noah's holding for my mother. "Sure," I reply, more for something to do than because I want a drink.

I follow him through to the kitchen, Jack at my heels, enjoying himself sniffing around this new place. Again, this room looks well-loved and well-used, with multiple dog-eared cookbooks on the shelves, racks of half-used herbs, and, when Charlie opens the fridge, multiple cuts of meat, colorful vegetables, and a variety of cheeses.

"She cooks," I say, with some surprise, I don't know why.

"She makes a mean Tandoori chicken." He retrieves two Diet Cokes, passes me one, and pops the top of his own. "Come and sit outside. She won't be long."

We go onto the deck and sit under the canopy in two comfortable deckchairs, while Jack goes off to explore the garden. "I didn't get a chance to see you at Noah's," Charlie says. "I'm so sorry to hear about your mom."

"Izzy and I got your flowers, thank you," I tell him. "Izzy was very touched by how many people sent them."

"Well, that's what they're for—showing those who are left behind that we're thinking of them."

I nod and give a little smile. It's been a really tough ten days. Izzy, especially, has gone through a whole gamut of emotions. Going through Mom's house and all her stuff was upsetting for both of us, because she'd kept so many items from our childhood, and so many of Dad's things—we never realized. It was good in many ways, a chance for us both to put our past to rest, and to reconnect just the two of us, as well. But we're both emotionally exhausted, and I think we're both tempted to sleep for a week once the reception is over today.

But first I need to see Poppy. I've had to put any notion of sorting out our relationship onto the backburner while I organized everything else, but although I haven't had much time to see her, she's always in my mind. I was hoping to catch up with her today once I'd said hello to everyone at Noah's, but not long after I spotted her, Noah came up to tell me she'd slipped out. He said Charlie had gone after her, and I suspected it was because she was upset. I'm not sure why—I suspect she's discovered she's not pregnant. I know I shouldn't have left the reception—it is for my mother, after all. But I couldn't let Poppy go through this without me. I was so convinced I'd knocked her up.

"Anyway," Charlie says, "I'd better get going and leave you two lovebirds to it."

So she's told him about us, then? That surprises me. I wonder if he knows all the details.

"Actually," I say, "I've got something to ask you... If you have a minute."

"Sure," he says.

I run a hand through my hair. "Er... It sounds as if Poppy has told you that we... ah... are sort of seeing each other."

He studies me for a moment, then leans back and rests an ankle on the other knee. I can't tell if he's wary or amused. "Yeah."

"Well... I'm incredibly fond of her... and we had a great time in Hawke's Bay. I haven't seen her much over the past week or so, but I've missed her a lot, and I thought... well, I hoped..." Jesus, I'm making a hash of this.

Charlie meets my gaze and his lips curve up.

"I'm doing my best," I say somewhat huffily, and his smile spreads.

"What do you want to ask me?" he says softly.

"Mr. King—"

"God, Charlie, please."

"Charlie... would I have your blessing to ask Poppy for her hand in marriage?"

He smiles. "Of course."

I feel a swell of relief and happiness. Jack comes back up to me as if sensing my emotions, and I pick him up and put him on my lap, kissing his head. "I haven't asked her yet, so it's entirely possible she'll say no."

"Well, you won't know until you ask."

"I think Daniel did a lot of damage."

His smile fades and his brow darkens. "I was all for going around to his house with a hammer to smash his kneecaps, but her mother talked me out of it."

That makes me laugh. "You'd have resorted to violence?"

"Probably not. But I'd like to have given him a piece of my mind. A grown man with a wife and two children seducing a younger woman, treating her badly, and then abandoning her... Yeah. Not impressed."

"Me neither. If you ever form a posse, give me a call."

We both smile.

"You're really serious about her," he says.

"I am. But I know she's been hurt, and she's reluctant to enter another relationship because of that."

"I didn't think I'd see her dating again for a long time," he admits. "Your suggestion you do things the old-fashioned way was very innovative."

I haven't blushed since I was about fourteen, but my face grows hot. "Uh…"

He tries not to laugh, and fails. "Sorry." He glances at the house, obviously sees Poppy coming out of the bathroom, and gets to his feet. "Look after my little girl, won't you?" he says softly. "She's pretty sweet on you."

I swallow and nod. We're shaking hands when Poppy comes out onto the deck.

"What's going on?" she asks suspiciously.

"Two men doing manly things," her father says. "I'm going to leave you to it. Are you okay?"

She nods. Her eyes are bright, and I suspect she's been crying, but she looks composed now. "Hey Jack," she says, bending to stroke him as he runs up to her.

"All right," Charlie says. "Come here." He gives her a big hug and a kiss on the forehead. "I'll see you soon, sweetheart. Let me know how it goes, okay?"

"Okay, Dad."

He nods at me, says goodbye to Jack, then walks into the house, and a few seconds later I hear the front door open and close.

"What are you doing here?" Poppy asks me softly. "You should be with Noah and your guests."

"I needed to see you," I tell her. "I was worried about you."

She studies her bare feet. She's painted her toenails a dark red. It makes me want to kiss them. "I'm sorry if I made you leave," she says. "I shouldn't have walked out without saying something. But I've been a bit emotional, and it all got too much for me."

"It's okay. It's not a problem." I move a little closer to her, slide a hand under her chin, and lift it so I can look into her eyes. "I want to apologize."

She swallows, her throat moving against my hand. "What for?"

"For not having seen you much the last ten days or so."

"It's okay, you've been busy and you lost your mom, it's perfectly understand—"

"Poppy," I say gently, "let me speak." I lower my hand and shove my hands in my pockets. "You're right, I have been preoccupied, but that's not a good enough excuse. I've missed you. And after what we shared at the lighthouse, you deserve so much more."

She drops her gaze and presses her lips together, I think to keep the bottom one from trembling.

"I'm crazy about you," I tell her simply. "I have been since I met you, and it's only gotten worse since we slept together. I knew it would. And I know you promised yourself you wouldn't fall for me, and that you don't want a relationship because you're worried about getting hurt again. But I want to tell you right now that if you let me, I'll treat you like a princess, and I'll worship the ground you walk on. I'll be by your side for the rest of our lives, and I'll love you and support you in whatever you want to do. I'll adore all the wonderful children I'm sure we'll have, and I'll work hard to make sure they have everything they need in life. I'll love you forever."

She looks up at me again, her eyes brimming with tears. "Marc…" she whispers.

But I haven't finished yet. I take my hands out of my pockets, extracting the velvet box there at the same time. I open it, revealing the diamond ring I bought down in Hamilton while I was there with Izzy.

"Poppy King," I say, "will you marry me and put up with my grouchy ways and make me the happiest man in the world?"

She stares at me, and her jaw drops. "Oh my God," she whispers.

I take her hand in mine and kiss her fingers.

"Did he tell you?" she asks me.

"Did who tell me what?"

She presses her fingers to her lips. "You really don't know?"

I frown, puzzled now. "Are you talking about Charlie? He said you were sweet on me. I hope he was right."

A tear runs down her cheek, and her fingers tremble. "Marc… I'm pregnant."

My eyes widen. "What?" I get hurriedly to my feet. "Are you sure?"

She nods. "I didn't think I was—I took a test and it was negative. It's why I left Noah's. I just felt so emotional thinking our… connection was over, and that it hadn't worked. But Dad made me take another test. He said I could have ovulated a day later than I thought, and he was right. The test was positive."

"Holy shit." I grin broadly. "We're having a baby?"

She hesitates, and my smile fades. "Don't," I say. "Don't tell me you want to have it without me." Oh Jesus. My heart is going to break if she says that.

SERENITY WOODS

She takes my hands in hers. "It's not that. It's just... If I say yes, I don't want you thinking it's only because I'm pregnant. That I'm frightened of having the baby alone. I need you to know I'm not marrying you because I feel I have to, you know?"

"Christ, Poppy, I don't care. I really don't. And I don't care who else knows. I love you, and if you love me, that's all that matters."

"I do love you," she says, tears running down her face. "I didn't mean to, but I do, I can't help it."

I lift the velvet box, take out the ring, and open my other hand to her. She places her left hand in it, and I slide the ring onto her finger.

Then I wrap her in my arms and give her a long, passionate kiss.

I only stop because she's crying so much. "Hey, come on," I murmur, wiping her cheeks with my thumbs. "This should be a happy moment."

"I am happy. Incredibly happy."

I kiss her again, and then kiss her cheeks, her nose, her eyelids, and back to her mouth. "Are we really having a baby?" I whisper, dropping a hand to her tummy.

"I know, I can't believe it either." She puts her hand over mine.

"It was that night," I say. "In the viewing room. I knew it. I felt it happen."

"You can't have," she scoffs, but her fingers curl around mine, and she presses our hands against her belly. "We can't tell anyone. Not for a few months. Miscarriages are very common in the early days."

"Yeah. It'll have to be our little secret." I kiss her again. "But you will marry me, won't you?"

"Yes, Marc. I'll marry you. But I'd like a quiet wedding. I don't want lots of pomp and fuss. Not like Izzy and Hal."

"Whatever you want. We can go away, just the two of us—all right, three of us," I add as Jack gives a short bark. "Or we could say our vows in a registry office and go for a meal afterward with your family."

"I'd like that. They'll be your family, too, you realize."

"Noah will be happy," I say, and she smiles.

She examines her ring for a moment. "It's so beautiful, Marc, thank you."

"I thought it was pretty," I tell her. The diamond isn't ginormous—I got one as big as I could afford, but it's set in an Art Deco Floral Halo, which I thought was suitable after our time in Napier.

160

"It's absolutely beautiful. Very me." She smiles, slides her arms around me, and looks into my eyes. "I had such a wonderful time at Hawke's Bay. Do you think it was because it was all so new?"

"No," I say, meaning it. "I think it was because we're so right for each other."

"I'm so sorry about your mom." She rests her cheek on my chest. "I wish she could be here to see you get married and to hold your baby."

Emotion washes over me, and for a moment I can't speak. I hold her tightly, looking out across the garden. I wish Mom could be here, too, and it makes me immensely sad to think neither she nor my father are around. But at least she's at peace now.

A *piwakawaka*, more commonly known as a fantail bird, swoops down onto the lemon tree nearest us. It jumps around from branch to branch almost as if it's dancing for us, displaying its beautiful tail. Mom liked fantails; in fact, I brought back a piece of artwork she had in her garden, made from a steel stencil design. I get the strange feeling she's trying to tell me she's still with me. I suppose she always will be, in my memories.

Jack runs down the steps to chase it, and it sits in the tree, as if it's laughing at his short legs.

We stand there like that for a long time, Poppy in my arms, warmed by the spring sunshine.

Chapter Twenty-Five

Poppy

Two weeks later, Marc and I get married.

There are only twenty-five of us present, including me and Marc. The Three Wise Men are there, with their wives. And all their children, natural or not, and their partners if they have them. And, of course, little baby Ethan, dressed in the cutest outfit of a onesie designed like a suit with a black bow tie printed at the top.

We say our vows at the local registry office, and I wear a simple cream dress and carry a bouquet of white roses, succulents, rosemary and sage, and paua shell, which is just beautiful. Marc wears a smart navy suit, and he has his hair trimmed, although not too much, because I like it long. He asks me to wear my hair up, because he wants to be the one to take it down when we go to bed that night, so my hairdresser braids it and pins it up with more fresh flowers.

Mom cries when she first sees me in the dress, and Dad conveniently gets something in his eye as he walks me down the aisle.

Our vows are simple, the whole process understated, and it just feels so right, I can't explain. Marc looks into my eyes as he promises to keep me in his heart for the rest of his life, and I believe every word he says.

For some reason, he also makes all the girls at the wedding cry. Nobody's going to have any mascara left intact by the end of the day.

After we're married, we have dinner at Between the Sheets on the seafront, and I spend a few hours dancing with my family and friends. It's only toward the end of the evening that I sit in one of the plastic chairs on the beach, where all the girls have finally crashed. The guys are up at the bar at the moment, talking rugby. We don't usually separate like this, but most of the guys aren't keen on dancing, and for once it's nice to spend some time with my girlfriends.

It's late now and the sun has set, but there's a beautiful warm November breeze blowing up from the ocean. The sea is the color of a fruit bowl full of plums, mandarins, peaches, and blueberries. We've eaten snapper caught this morning, and I've had a small glass of champagne, and I feel warm, content, and happy.

"My feet feel twice their size," Jules complains, circling her feet at the ankles.

"And they weren't small to begin with," Nix comments.

"Gee, thanks." Jules pokes her tongue out and we all laugh. It's true that, because she's tallish at five-nine, her feet aren't particularly dainty, but she hardly needs clown shoes.

I stretch and yawn. "I'm going to sleep so well tonight. I'm knackered."

"Don't let Fitz hear you say that," Clio says. "I think he's hoping to keep you up for a few more hours." She smirks, and the others chuckle.

I just give a smile. I have a man of my own who loves me, and for once I can feel smug. "My husband is welcome to entertain me any way he wants."

Clio huffs a sigh. "I can't believe you're all settling down. Jules, we'll have to found a losers club."

"Thanks, Clio."

"No offence."

"None taken," Jules says. "I'm happy being single. It's liberating, and my time is my own, and I don't have anyone to tell me what to do… and oh my God I'm so desperate to get laid I can't tell you."

We all burst out laughing, and she covers her face with her hands. "I miss sex so much," she says with a sigh. "I'm so envious of you all I could die."

"I've got shares in Duracell," Clio says, "I get through so many of their batteries."

"Oh God, Clio, TMI," Izzy states.

She pouts. "I'm with Jules. I hate you all."

"You need to get out more," I tell her. "All you do is work, Clio. Now you're qualified, maybe you can take your foot off the pedal and socialize a bit."

"Not if Stefan has his way," she grumbles. Stefan's the head of the veterinary center, and she's often complained that he's a slave driver. "I swear, if I left early, that Viking would run out and drag me back by my hair." She purses her lips. "Not that that would necessarily be a bad thing."

"Oh…" Nix says. "Got the hots for the sexy vet, have you?"

"He's gorgeous," Clio admits. "I'm thinking of asking him out for a drink. Maybe if I write an invite in runes he'll think about it."

"I know what you're doing," Jules says mildly, "and it's not going to work."

"Told you," Clio says to Nix. "She's too wise to fall for your dastardly plot."

I smile. I know Jules likes Stefan, and that she's been angling for a date with him for some time. So far, though, he's studiously avoided her. None of us is sure why. She's lovely—bright, bubbly, and sexy in a girl-next-door kinda way. Mind you, I have seen a couple of the women he's dated in the past, and they've all been like models, near to six foot and stunningly beautiful, so maybe she's just not his type.

"I'm moving on," Jules says. "He's not interested in me, and that's fine. It's about time I focused my laser-beam-like gaze elsewhere. Like William the groundskeeper."

We all laugh—William is about seventy-five and has about two hairs on his head.

"What about you?" I ask Clio. "Got your eye on anyone?"

She shrugs. "Nope."

"Liar," Remy says in her beautiful French accent. "I saw you ogling Ryan the other day."

Clio's eyes widen. "Ogling? Jesus, Remy, where do you learn these words?"

"Albie teaches me. And do not change the subject. You were looking at his butt when he bent over the table."

"He has a nice butt," Clio protests, ignoring our sniggers. "Very tight. A girl can window shop, can't she?"

"Are you interested in him?" I ask her. He's quite a catch. He's Hal's and Jules's half-brother, adopted by Brock King when he met their mother, Erin. He's three years older than me, and I've known him all my life, as our fathers have always spent a lot of time together. By the time Clio was in her teens, though, Ryan had left home, so I guess she doesn't know him as well as I do. When he was younger, he was never without a girlfriend, although he was faithful to his ex-wife, as far as I know. His recent divorce was a tough one, and has left him reluctant to date again, so he's thrown himself into his work.

"I'd do him tomorrow," Clio admits, making us all laugh. "I've had a crush on him for years."

"Really?" Jules looks amused. "I never knew."

"Well I've never acted on it," Clio says. "For Reasons, with a capital R."

"What kind of reasons?" Nix asks. "He's single. His divorce came through at Christmas."

"I know," Clio says. "He's my cousin, though."

"By adoption," Nix replies. "And anyway, it's not illegal to marry your first cousin in New Zealand. It's not in many places. Charles Darwin married his first cousin, Emma Wedgwood."

Clio blinks at that information. "Ryan is also eight years older than me."

"Noah's ten years older than me," Abby comments. She's been quiet, listening while she nurses Ethan, but he's now in his carry-seat, and she raises her eyebrows to challenge the younger girl.

"Yeah," Clio says. "True. But you and Noah are so well suited. Ryan's... I don't know, mature. Confident. I get all tongue-tied with him."

"You, tongue-tied?" Jules laughs.

"I do," Clio protests. "I can never think what to say."

"Flash your boobs at him," Nix says. "That'll do the trick." She gestures at where Clio's blouse is unbuttoned to show an inch of cleavage. She's a D cup, with a tiny waist and wide hips, your typical hourglass, so she tends to draw a lot of male attention, especially with her blonde hair.

"Ha!" Clio rolls her eyes. "Anyway, I can't imagine he'd be interested in me. His ex was so elegant and composed. She was a lawyer, for Christ's sake. Really intelligent."

"You're a vet," Izzy points out. "You're hardly dumb."

"Yeah, but I'm, like, blah, blah, blah all the time. I'm too in your face. He's very quiet."

"He wasn't when he was younger," Jules states. "He was quite the lad."

"Really?" Clio's eyebrows rise.

Jules sips her wine with a knowing smirk, glances around, then leans forward conspiratorially. We all lean forward with her. "I overheard him arguing with his ex once," she whispers. "Samantha called him 'insatiable' and said she was fed up with him trying to wear her out."

"Ooh," we all say, and Clio's jaw drops.

"Wow," she says, looking over at him. "Really?"

All the girls' eyes widen. The knowledge that he's secretly a sex god is a revelation to everyone here.

"That's it," Nix announces. "Clio's homed in on him. Like a guided missile, about to blow him out of the water."

"Clio's not allowed to blow anyone while I'm still single," Jules states, prompting us all to erupt into laughter. "Sorry," she adds as we descend into giggles, "I've drunk too much champagne. That's your fault, Poppy. This is really good stuff."

"I'm glad you're enjoying it." I've only had a small glass, topping it up with lemonade so hopefully nobody notices.

I lift my face to the sea breeze and sigh. "Thank you all for coming tonight. I've had such a wonderful day."

"Aw," Izzy says, "I'm so pleased you got your happily-ever-after. You deserve it."

"You too," I tell her, and we reach out and hold hands for a moment. She's officially my sister-in-law now, and we've been spending quite a lot of time together over the past two weeks, talking about her and Marc's mom. She's given me a lot of insight into their childhood, which has helped me understand him more, and I think she's appreciated being able to talk about the problems she had with her mom with someone other than Hal.

"What's going on over here?" Marc says, approaching with the rest of the guys. "There's far too much fun being had without us."

"We're talking about Clio being a guided missile," I begin, then laugh as she shoots daggers at me. "Come on," I say, taking Marc's hand. "Dance with me."

I lead him back to the small dance floor, and lift my arms around his neck as he pulls me close. Around me, some of the others also start dancing, and I sigh and give him a dreamy smile.

"Having a good time?" he murmurs, bending to kiss my nose.

"Wonderful. I'm trying to fix Jules and Clio up," I tell him. "I want everyone to be as happy as I am."

"Aw." He bends his head and kisses my lips. "I'm so glad you're not regretting marrying me."

That makes me laugh. "Not at all. I'm so happy, Marc. I love you so much."

"I love you too." He glances down at my belly. "And little Fitz."

I giggle and glance around. "Shh."

"You still haven't told anyone?"

I shake my head. "I want to wait until I'm three months. It's our secret. I still can't quite believe it."

"Me either. It's so funny to think there's a little person growing inside you."

"Your little person," I whisper, looking up into his eyes.

"My little person. And now you're my woman." He takes my hand from behind his neck and shows me my wedding ring. "I've branded you. So every man will know you belong to me. Do you mind?"

"No," I say honestly.

He releases my hand and lowers his hand back to my hips, pulling me close. "And tonight I'm going to brand you in another way. I'm going to write my name all over you, on every inch of your skin, so you never forget whose girl you are."

"How could I forget?" I lift my face to his for a kiss. "You're the only man for me, Marc Fitzgerald. Till death do us part."

Newsletter

If you'd like to be informed when my next book is available,
you can sign up for my mailing list on my website,
http://www.serenitywoodsromance.com

About the Author

USA Today bestselling author Serenity Woods writes sexy contemporary romances, most of which are set in the sub-tropical Northland of New Zealand, where she lives with her wonderful husband.

Website: http://www.serenitywoodsromance.com
Facebook: http://www.facebook.com/serenitywoodsromance